Street
Queens

KURT ANTHONY

Published by Anthony Entertainment and Pages On Fire Press
www.streetqueens.org
www.Facebook.com/KurtAnthonyStreetQueens

ISBN-13: 978-0615681207

ONE

Dear God,

I'm writing you this letter, because I know that you are wise, compassionate, all knowing, and the one who will understand me. I'm writing to tell you my story, so when I die, which I think will be soon, you will let me into Your house when I come knocking at your door. I'm a sixteen year old black female from Harlem, which I called Hellem. They call me TKO Dear God, because I enjoy banging mothafuckas until they're almost out; stunned, battered, bloody, but still conscious, so they know who hit 'em. In boxing that's a "technical knock out," so that's who I am, TKO. I'm a double barrel toting, four blunt smoking a day, let it all hang out in yo and yo Momma's face gang banger 24/7.

   I confess, Dear God, even my dreams are not like everybody else's dreams. My dreams are only about blood, mayhem, and shadows in the dark. I hope you see now why, I'm writing you this letter. When I die, please don't let me go to those shadows in the dark. Don't let me lie too long in a dark, cold, damp grave, surrounded by a city of born again hood niggas, who drowned swimming in oceans of misery. I'm tired of being a rolling stone, but I barely sleep. When I close my eyes I hear voices whispering at my grave. I'm crooked in my soul now, Dear God. I was a straight A student, an avid reader and probably one of the smartest in my school, but surely the most troubled. My math teacher, who noticed my agitation as I tore through equation after equation, told me to study yoga and meditation and to practice it because that would help me relax and keep calm. I'm reading a book she gave me, The Autobiography Of A Yogi, by Paramahansa Yogananda. He is one of the great emissaries of India's ancient wisdom. But that ancient wisdom don't mean shit in the ghetto and Yogananda can't help me pistol whip these bitches! I'm TKO and this is my story.

Maybe what makes me so cold is that I've been on my own almost forever. My so called mother went away when I was six and the only person who cared about me died years ago. I live with my uncle, but he only tolerates me because I work in his rackets and I only work for him because it's nasty to sleep on the street. So I made my own family in the ghetto way. I created a gang and sold it to other lost souls by hyping the organization as the coldest, boldest, crew on the street.

It was not far from midnight, on New Year's Eve 2010, when I begin initiating mothafuckas into my gang. Street Queens is what I call my all girl gang. War Dogs G-Gang is the name of my male gang. I need Alpha male dogs to go after and give the beat down to rival male gangs. The initiation took place inside a tunnel in an empty dark place in Harlem, not far from the Hudson River. The sounds of gun shots, or maybe fireworks, echoed in the distance, accompanied by the squeaks and scratches of rats getting their party on inside the tunnel. I felt the tension coming from my crew, waiting at an abandoned car near the tunnel opening. Here's how it went down. They're gathering their nerves, deciding who's going to walk inside first.

I slowly load my Spring Amory XDM 9mm, counting the bullets. My sweaty hands put the mag loader inside the handle of the gun and I adjust the target sights. I lean down to a green army duffel bag and remove an old, beat up dirty bullet proof vest that I bought from the same supplier my uncle uses. I call that vest the Old Rugged Cross, which I named after a song my great grandmama used to sing to me when we walked to church on Sundays. You see, Dear God, I was raised by her until she died when I was only six years old. I loved her with all my heart. She provided me with the only stable home I ever had. I loved everything about her. She was a righteous woman. She prayed with me our knees before she tucked me in each night. She was always singing and cooking. My great grandmama cooked the best tasting meals I ever had. I especially loved her fried chicken, mashed potatoes, greens, mac and cheese, candy yams, smothered pork chops, chocolate cake and hot chocolate milk. Before she took me to Sunday school she dressed me in beautiful soft dresses, with printed flowers. I would put my nose to the flowers to smell the freshness of the dress. Then I would watch her in the mirror tying ribbons in my hair, ribbons that looked like rainbows dancing in the sky. Easter Sunday was one of my favorite days, because I would get a brand new dress, new shoes, and matching ribbons for my hair. I also would get to write and recite a poem in church on Easter Sunday. I still remember that last poem I wrote before she died.

"I love the Lord, like I love great grandma. I pray, she and the Lord would never leave me alone. I hope her food would always taste good and that we will eat dinner every night at the same time. And I will always be a good girl and do what great grandma say, each and every day."

I hear someone walking inside the tunnel and I hear the rats' celebration. I see my 19 year old cockdiesel, mule jaw, big teeth, pretty boy, approaching. He's the ghetto Valentino. I've seen bitches go at each other with box cutters, fighting over this nigga. But don't let that pretty face of his fool you, Dear God. He rose from the hellish mean streets of Jersey City. They should give Jersey City a new brand name, "Murder, Misery, Suffering And Thank God I Escaped To This Grave." If they ever named streets after murderers, he boasts, he would be right there at the top of the list, a grave digger so prolific, he says, he wears two shovels on his back like a cross. He leans down and picks up the Old Rugged Cross, but despite his bravado I can smell the fear on his breath. I can see in his eyes he wishes for another life, to be in another place, and in another time and space. But he knows as well I that will happen only in death. You can feel by his tremble that he knows that he could be moments away from finding out what could be on that other side. And if he dies tonight, will his own demons await him on the other side of that door?

He straps the Old Rugged Cross on his chest. The reason I gave the vest that name is because the bullet proof vest is the symbol of my generation's Old Rugged Cross. It's the symbol of the pathology that hangs over every ghetto in America, like a blood cloud, pregnant with black rain, releasing a venomous poison in every drop that falls. I can see the vision now, an endless sea of black youth standing in the rain, heads toward the sky, mouths open wide.

He takes a few steps backwards looking me in the eyes and says with a heart filled with rage and pain, "My name is 9-mm-Rottweiler and I kill way mo' niggas than the Klan!" He yells, pounding his chest like his first cousin, the silver back Congo gorilla. I raise my 9mm, Jericho up to his chest. The butt of the gun feels like ice, the trigger like fire. My hand is sweating and freezing at the same time. One side of my body is on fire, the other side is colder than ice. I hear a voice crying out from Jericho. "Don't do it. Don't let my dick get on a hard and make me start coming!"

Then I hear another voice in my head, much darker and more sinister than Jericho's.

"Pull the trigger now! In the ghetto this is how a boy becomes a man."

It feels like pliers are choking my finger down hard on the trigger. I need air but there's none to breathe. A window shattering bang is heard as a bolt of lightening rockets out the barrel of my gun. Jericho kicks back with the viciousness of a 200 pound jackhammer. The force of the impact of 9-mm-Rottweiler hitting the ground seems to have opened up the earth, shooting him straight down to hell. I hear rats crying. I look down and see a huge bull rat screaming, standing on his hind legs, next to 9-mm-Rottweiler's, lifeless body. The bull rat runs inside the vest, digging into 9-mm-Rottweiler's chest. My boy begins to wake from the dead, as if the bull rat were performing an exorcism. He jumps up off the ground tearing the vest away. He screams like a bitch when he sees the rat clinging to his chest. I run over, knocking the rat off his chest. He has already forgotten he just got shot in the chest, asking, as if he's just seen a ghost, "Did he bite me? Did he bite me?"

Next on the greatest hit list is my girl Missy Capone, who named herself after an ugly, deadly, character in the movie "The Untouchables," not even knowing that Al Capone was a real gangster bootlegger. Missy is an 18 year old caramel colored tomboy with droopy, sleepy eyes, and red hair beneath a baseball cap. She enters the tunnel wearing a black leather jacket, baggy jeans I know she stole on 125 Street and construction boots. She grew up in one foster home after the other. Now she's aged out into the streets. She's flashing her crooked smile. This crazy bitch shows no fear. I guess she figures with her kind of life, it makes no differences whether she's dead or alive. She leans down and lifts that Old Rugged Cross. She puts it on, steps back and says with that damn crooked ass smile of hers "War Dogs, Street Queens. It's time I look my killa in the eye." Jericho seems to rise up on his own. He whispers in my ears, "Now that you got my dick on a hard I'm ready to come again!" I pull the trigger and the bullet lifts her off the ground. She falls hard. A few moment later she coughs up blood. Big Wolf, 18 and ugly, enters the tunnel. He picks Missy Capone off the ground removing the vest and puts it on. The left side of his mouth is in a upward frown, like he is smelling something bad. He steps back and says, "I'm Big Wolf. I specialize in murder and extortion! War Dogs G-Gang." I pull the trigger and this nigga don't even move. I'm unsure what to do next, because I've never seen no shit like this. Usually mothafuckas roll like dominoes when they catch a fire in the chest. I'm afraid to shoot this gorilla again. The next shot might kill him. I hear Jericho say, "fuck it" before he starts blasting again. Big Wolf is finally blown to the ground. I run up to him and the vest is smoking. I call his name, reaching down for him. He opens his eyes pushing my hand away and growls, "Get the fuck away from me." I'm overcome with joy to see my nigga alive. He rolls up easy and drops the vest to the ground.

Scarface Pretty, a slim, fine, bitch is standing in front of me, wearing that Old Rugged Cross.

"I'm Scarface Pretty, Scarface, like the man in the poster in every gangsta's bedroom. I'm the symbol of the collapse of law and order in the streets. War Dogs Street Queens. I send mothafuckas, to ghetto hell or heaven, makes no diff to me."

I pull the trigger and blow this bitch up off the ground into next year, if not the next life. She lies on the ground motionless as my fine light skinned Puerto Rican lover enters the tunnel. She's a freak and it makes me angry. She goes both ways. She says she's in love with me, but she also needs some real dick too, on the side. I explain to her do what you need to do, but just don't bring those dick heads around me. Being in this bitch's presence is starting to get my pussy dripping wet. I can even feel Jericho's dick getting hard. Scarface Pretty regains consciousness, putting the vest next on Switchblade. Our girl is fast and slim as the knife she named herself after, but little Switchblade almost disappears in the large vest. She takes a deep breath, trying to control her fear. I look at her like, "are you sure you want to do this?" But we both know there is no turning back. She nods let's go, almost hyperventilating.

"I'm Switchblade and I rob mo' mothafuckas than Wall Street. And I pledge to the Street Queens' flag, that I will rob ever bodega from Spanish Harlem to uptown Dominican Republic."

I shoot this bitch in the chest and the shock waves run down my body. That makes me want to fuck this bitch right here in this tunnel. I walk over to her still body, kneel down and kiss her on her cold lips. The bitch don't seem to be breathing, so I kiss her some more. She slowly regains consciousness. I help her to her feet removing that Old Rugged Cross. She quickly moves away, beginning to throw up. I thank God for that, because for a moment, I thought the freak was dead and good pussy is a terrible thing to waste.

Jamaican Bonnie slowly walks inside the tunnel, another sexy ass bitch, with soft chocolate skin, clear olive shaped big eyes, soft cotton juicy lips that remind me of heart shaped valentine candy. She has a tiny diamond in the most beautiful nose, a nose that I wish I had. We found that pretty bitch through our outreach program. You see, gangs all over New York are starting to recruit good girls, from good, stable families, on their way to college and all. Bonnie comes from an upper middle class, elite Jamaican family who owns hotels here and in Jamaica. Matter of fact, she's the only person who I ever met whose family has a big house in the Hamptons. You see, she's like that girl Tayshana Murphy, the promising basketball star who was on her way to college then on to the WNBA before she got caught up in gang war between two crews and got gunned down. We recruited Jamaican Bonnie right in front of her private high school full of white kids. It didn't take much, everyone wants to belong to something greater than themselves. And comfortable girls like Bonnie think it will be fun to slum for a while, play the gangsta, walk on the wild side. It's a kick for them, like E. Within a week we had this virgin Jamaican bitch holding guns for us and eating more funky pussy than Condoleezza Rice and those nappy headed bitches in the WNBA.

I aim Jericho toward her chest. This child don't even look right in that vest. She appears to be in shock, the tears on her face frozen in time. I hear Jericho starting to laugh at me and I think I see my great grandma walk inside the tunnel, singing the "Old Rugged Cross." And who is that man over there pointing at me in the shadows? I see him, but nobody else notices anything. I look at Jamaican Bonnie and she is wearing my face. She looks exactly like me standing there wearing that old Rugged Cross. Still, no one else seems to see what I see. I look at her and see that every place a tear drop falls on the ground, a flower grows. The man in the shadows points at me, then at the flowers on my grave. I just want to cut off my ears and take out my eyes. I can't stand the sound of Jericho laughing at me. I close my eyes in the pitch black darkness so I can see. "Is that you great grandma, watching over me?" I whisper, so no one else hears. I pull the trigger, but hear no sound. When I open my eyes there's great grandma standing in front of me. She is holding Jamaican

Bonnie's hand, but Bonnie is a little girl now. They walk away, as great grandma starts to sing.

I turn and my whole crew is standing around me, except for Switchblade, who's leaning over Jamaican Bonnie's lifeless body. Switchblade shakes her, calls her name. Blood flows from the back of Bonnie's head where she cracked it open when she fell from the impact. That's what must have killed her.

Switchblade cries out "Oh my God she's dead. She's not breathing."

Did I just see that bitch open her eyes and smile at me? I'm thinking, "Damn this girl didn't have a bad bone in her body." But yet she had the baddest karma of us all tonight. Damn that's fucked up. Her mother will never see her graduate from high school and college and grow into a woman. She will never see her laugh or cry again, or cry herself at her daughter's wedding. She will never ever get to see her on the shores of Jamaica again, unless it's in a black box, draped in sheets of eulogies. I pray that the innocent blood won't flow through the cracks in the coffin. Amen. I think I know now what great grandma meant when she used to sing the song "Old Rugged Cross." Every human on the planet, including Jesus himself, one day carries that Old Rugged Cross.

On a hill far away stood an Old Rugged Cross
The Emblem of suffering and shame
And I love that old Rugged Cross
Where the dearest and best
For a world of lost sinners was slain

Switchblade is beating on Bonnie's chest just trying to revive her, but Bonnie is dead. "What we gonna do?"

I don't say a word because I don't know what to do. I never thought about somebody dying during gang initiation. What can I do? I can't call the police. I can't call the mother or father. Can't call the school. I can't even call you tonight, Dear God, cause obviously nobody's home. Big Wolf steps forward and says in a dead monotone voice "She was just telling me yesterday that she was gonna die young. If she does, bury her in a bed of roses."

I reach into my pocket and take out a five hundred dollar bill, handing it to Big Wolf. "You know what to do with this." I look down at Switchblade and tell her to man up, as the rats bring in the new year, howling like wolves. About 45 minutes later, Big Wolfe meets us down by the river carrying a king's ransom in roses and a white sheet. We spread it on the ground and Missy Capone, Scarface Pretty, and Switchblade cover it with rose petals. We lay Jamaican Bonnie's stiffening body on the roses and wrap her up in the shroud, like a baby in bunting. We all bow our heads. I say a soft prayer over her body.

"Come down dear Lord, and take your child by the hand. Put her close to you. Hug her tight in your arms. Take her up to your house, that place beyond the sky. Tell her, Dear Lord, that You will never let her go. And that her pain and suffering on this earth is no more. Give her momma and daddy, the strength to carry on. Let them know that their only child is in a better place. In Your name, Amen."

Big Wolfe and 9-mm-Rottweiler, pick up Bonnie's dead body and swing her back and forth building momentum. They throw her body into the black river. As it hits the water a chill convulses me and midnight strikes. Loud bangs, sounds like gunshots, people celebrating. Huge, bright fire works explode in the sky, reflected in the river over Bonnie's floating body. Laughter and party music stream across the water. My body is warm now, I feel happy and free. I look up and see beautiful fire works exploding everywhere across the sky. I can see millions of glittering stars falling to earth from the explosions. "Oh wow, look at this." As the stars rain down all around us they turn into beautiful roses. "Bonnie, can you see'em? Can you see all the beautiful roses raining down on us? Look how they float like petals in the water. Can you see them? God is opening the door to his kingdom for you." Everyone stares as I float off into a world of my own. I turn and see a glowing figure in the dark walking in our direction, as I hear one hundred angels' voices singing. As the glowing figure gets closer I can see it's Paramahansa Yogananda walking towards us. His face is soft and beautiful. He has long black metallic hair resting on his shoulders and he seems to almost float in his white metallic robe. Yogananda walks up to me and smiles. He takes my hands and kisses my trigger finger. I can feel his spiritual master Swami Sri Yukteswar Giri around me. I look at Bonnie's body in the river and the floating roses around her are glowing like candles. Yogananda kisses me on my forehead before walking away. He walks into the river, walking on water to Bonnie's body, lifting her and walking in the direction of the Eastern God. It looks as if he's walking on exploding fire works. I raise my arms out wide as the beautiful roses rain down. I see Bonnie and Yogananda disappear as I hear holy men's humming voices carried by the wind. The colorful roses pile up like snow around us as they turn into candle light on the dark, murky, muddy, waters.

TWO

Dear God,

I'm overwhelmed. This time my fuck up can't be fixed. This TKO character I created, she's a fantasy, but I let her get out of control. I lost my real self, my Jean self in the role of gangsta and Bonnie is dead and I'm responsible. But if I let myself think about it I'll go crazy. I have to man up and figure out how to protect my crew. Anyway, I'm part of the Harlem streets and in the streets there's no conscience. Here you're either predator or prey. Have mercy, Dear God, on Bonnie, who never should have left her comfort zone and on me, who never had one.

I live with my Great Uncle Miles and his girl friend Pinch. He's a numbers runner and numbers banker, and he operates out of our apartment. I work for him collecting numbers all over Harlem when I'm not in school or running my drug business in the lobby of my building. Numbers running in my family goes back a long way, back to the glory days of the gritty underworld of Harlem. When I first came to live with Uncle Miles he sat me down to tell me a story. I was expecting a fairy tale, or a Bible story like great grandmama used to tell me. But Miles' story was the history of the family business, the numbers.

"Once upon a time," Miles said, the numbers game was created by a highly intelligent brother named Casper Holstein, who made millions of dollars back in the 30's running the numbers business in Harlem. He worked as a janitor on Wall Street and began studying the Federal Reserve Clearing House report number totals in the paper. The betting scheme was all based on the closing daily results of the New York Stock Exchange. The winning total number paid 600 to one. By having the numbers recorded every day in the newspaper cheating was avoided. Back then you could bet on a number any and everywhere; on street corners, bars, barber shops, beauty parlors, corner stores, drug houses, "Hell," miles said, sometimes even in church. Whatever the winning number was for that day the info would be given to the banker who collected the money and paid who ever won. They tell me my grandmama was one of the best and brightest, the most prolific talented super stars in the number running game. She was to the numbers game what Iron Mike Tyson was to the fight game, a knock out specialist. The numbers banker she worked for couldn't even get up from her punch and figure out how she did it. She had figured out a system to calculate what the winning numbers would be, before they came out in the paper that day. She would hit the numbers the way LeBron James hit jumpers, all up in your face. So the banker she worked for couldn't do a damn thing about it, other then get his ass knocked the fuck out.

Damn, it's Friday night. Friday night is poker party night and I hear the noise as soon as I step off the elevator. Most of the folks there are not there for poker. They are there for the party within the party, the cheap drinks, the coke and the two dollar shots. A thick cloud of cigarette and weed smoke greets me at the door without saying hello. Bobby Womack's song "Across 110 St." is blasting off the walls.

> The family on the other side of town,
> Would catch hell without a ghetto around
> In every city you find the same thing going down
> Harlem is the capital of every ghetto in town

People are everywhere, sitting, standing, perching on the arms of chairs, lounging on the floor. In one corner there is a group smoking weed. In the next, cocaine is on the menu. The corner next to me I can't even mention. In the corner that's left, they're doing it all, drinking, smoking and snorting. More hoods are sitting around on cheap velvet furniture bought from the back of a truck of all stolen goods. The furniture looks a lot like all of Miles' cheap gaudy looking clothes, also bought out of the back of a truck. He's a very good looking man, tall, strong, with thick, black, curly Indian hair that matches his dark chocolate complexion. He has a perfect mustache, a beautiful mouth and a mountainous smile that seems to glow in the dark. But if you piss this crazy Negro off he turns into Count Dracula in a blink of an eye.

That's exactly what he believes in, an eye for a eye and a tooth for a tooth. These niggas know not to loose their minds up in here, because they will loose their lives if they try to fuck with that crazy Negro or his money. He's the only person on the planet that I think I'm afraid of. I remember walking down the street one night with him when I was a child. These two black men and a Hispanic dude, tried to rob him when he had just collected the numbers money. The dud that came up behind him, his throat was cut out with a sawed off machete. The two men in front were chopped down as they tried to turn and run. One dude fell in front of a drain and you could hear his blood pouring into the sewer. Underneath his poker table in the middle of the living room Miles has hidden not only that same sawed off machete, but a sawed off shot gun as well, so none of these hoods in here want Count Dracula coming at them with a sawed off shot gun in the left hand and a sawed off machete in the right.

His girl friend Pinch, on the other hand, is no beauty queen. This bitch is short, bow legged, with thin hair, eyes damn near crossed, and skinny legs that end in flat bad feet. If I didn't know any better I would think that she was a gnome from another planet, but the last I checked the United States don't issue visas to alien gnomes, so I'm assuming she's part human. To be honest, with make up and her weave she doesn't look so bad, but I see Pinch when she gets up in the morning. Lord have mercy! I like Pinch though, she looks like a hood , but she tries to act like a lady and she's very nice and sweet to me. Which is probably why handsome Miles is with her. They go way back. He trusts her and the sounds coming from their bedroom some nights explain it all.

I walk over to the poker table where Miles is drinking and playing poker with his friends, Mo Jackson, an old G in this 50's and Catfish, a man so ugly he looks to me like a black, 6 feet, 250 pound rubber lipped swamp cat fish. He thinks everyone calls him Catfish because that's his favorite eating fish. Whatever. I don't get too close to him because tonight, like every night the smells of catfish and liquor leak from every pore in his body. For a change Catfish is gloating.

"I got your catfish looking ass now. Go ahead and put it down." He laughs at Miles, "What you got to say now big boy?"

"You the one they call Catfish. I'm the one who got your ass now," Miles says.

"Have you been drinking that moonshine liquor again? You ain't won shit all night. You may be a big time numbers banker, but I'm the big boss in the house tonight. Prepare to start crying again."

"I don't give a damn how much you've won. You're in my house paying me to drink my liquor, you gonna spend all your money on liquor here tonight like you always do."

Mo Jackson laughs and says with a smile, "You know that's right."

"Shut the fuck up you alligator lookin mothafucka," Catfish shouts back.

Miles looks up at me and grabs my hand and asks "How was school today?"

"It was Okay."

"Are you hungry? I have some fried chicken, peas and rice and some greens on the stove in the kitchen."

"Sounds good."

"Can I get back to this ass whipping?" Catfish asks Miles

Before I'm out of the room Cat fish starts talking about me.

"That grand niece of yours look just like a grand nephew. My mama always said it's not what you do but how you do it. Everybody knows that in the Black church the choir director is gay, but they didn't walk around acting and talking like Madea. You see these young girls walking around Harlem holding hands who look like a cross between Mike Tyson and a crocodile. If you walking around with a hardcore butch who looks like a bastard version of a man, you might as well get yourself a real man."

I don't pay any attention to all that and don't give a shit about these fucked up ass, old Gees. Matter of fact I don't give a damn about much, right now except to be one of

Harlem's rising premier gang bangers. If I don't focus on that I'm lost. I walk into the kitchen and the first thing I see is Pinch and a big ass cockroach running towards me screaming "Help, get me away from this ugly bitch!" I just hope he didn't eat up all the fried chicken and greens because his ass is fat, looking as though he's been standing on the stove with a plate in his hands eating with Pinch all night. I crush the cocksucker with my boot as he's passes by me wiping the grease from his mouth. He'll be back soon as a ghost, I'm sure.

"Hey what's going on? Here comes my favorite baby girl," Pinch says with a smile, "You hungry, baby?" she asks, hugging me.

"Yeah I am, I'm starving matter of fact. I hear we have some chicken and greens."

"Nothing but some good food and some good love here for you tonight" she says opening the pots, "The fried chicken is warm, but I need to heat up the rice, peas and greens for you. Give me a minute. Me and Miles is going upstate to see your mother this weekend and she wants you to come with us."

What she just said pisses me off, but I try to control my emotions.

"I don't have time to roll upstate this weekend. I have a lot of stuff to do and a lots of homework to catch up with for school. Plus I have some tests in school next week, I need to study for."

She looks at me as if she doesn't believe me.

"I know it's been hard for you not having her there for you, but she is still your mother no matter what. I know she had a lot of demons and was addicted to the streets. Despite all of her human flaws she really loves you. I don't think a day goes by, she doesn't wish she could turn back the hands of time."

"Tell her I said good luck with that. I'm not going upstate sitting on some bus for hours just to see her with an army of females like her, wearing those pajamas all day. What kind of shit is that? Grown ass woman walking around all day in pajamas?"

"Honey, you have a right to be angry. Your mama never thought about you when she was running the streets. Shit, she never thought about anybody. She never thought. She lived from high to high; alcohol to weed, weed to coke, coke to crack, crack to sex with anyone who'd buy more crack. That's who she was. But that's not who you have to be. And I know honey that's where you're going with these gangs of yours. TKO. Really? Is that what great grandmama wanted for you? You have a brain baby. Use it to find something better. All this hate and rage only poisons you. Otherwise you'll only turn out like your mama, maybe even worse. Find your heart.

I know you'll never like your mama, but pity her. She's lost and she knows it. You still have a chance to find yourself."

"You're a good person Pinch, but you can't even protect me from Miles. He's had me running the streets since before I wore a bra. That's my life. I'm too deep in the game. I don't feel pity for my mama. I feel heartache, headache and pain."

I hate Mondays. And this Monday morning is worse than usual. I have a throbbing headache from a bad cold getting worse, but I have to I get my ass up out of bed anyway if I don't want to fail everything because of truancy. I just have time to shower, oil my braids and grab a bag of barbecue chips for breakfast.

I'm so busy on 126th Street coughing my brains out and thinking I should have stayed home in bed, that I almost don't notice the big black puffy jacket, hoodie wearing, young goon following me down the street. I know I'm walking through the jungle, but why in hell is he following me? I'm on my way to school and don't have any money on me from collecting numbers. So what the hell is going on? I look back and suddenly a black SUV with tinted black windows speeds up the street, in my direction. I see the young goon on the phone and hear him say, "hurry up." This shit doesn't feel right I'm thinking. This cold is kicking my ass and my head feels like it's about to fall off my shoulders and bounce on the sidewalk. I walk past a live chicken factory that smells like rotting corpses, making me feel even more nauseous. The black SUV is beside me. It stops for a second but starts again. Shit. It's following me. I look around and realize there's not a person in sight except the young goon. I reach into my coat for Jericho, but of course I don't carry him to school. I feel my heart pounding down to my wrists. Jesus. Something is about to go down and I'm a sitting duck out here in a jungle of hungry wolves. I look back and the gorilla is looking directly at me and walking a lot faster in my direction. I try to look cool as I glance around for an escape. I hasten my pace but the gorilla accelerates. The SUV's side window rolls down slowly. Oh shit! It's that bitch I've been seeing in my sleep. It's Kim, the 19 year bitch who's the head of the notorious Gun Runnin Divas. They have a reputation for taking their victims to dark basements and torturing them. It's very effective intimidation. I have a fear of the dark unless I've created the scene, like in my tunnel, so I take off running.

I'm running like there's rocket boosters on my feet, when I hear a gunshot and a bullet bouncing off the building next to me. I run to the corner and turn and run to 125th St. I hear the SUV not far behind me. I look back and the goon is directly behind me about to grab me. I knew I should have stayed my ass in bed this morning. I could have been in bed now eating Hot Pockets watching reruns of the Kardashians.

But that would've been too relaxing I guess. I'm about to get caught up into some bullshit, like a ship wreck at sea. I'm about to be tortured in a dark, black basement, my worst nightmare. I look around and the gorilla is within arm's reach of me. I stop abruptly, dropping to my knees and the gorilla crashes into me, flipping over on the sidewalk. I stagger up like a punch drunk fighter and run across the street toward C Town, the grocery store. I hear another gunshot. A bullet whistles over my head. I'm thinking that I might not ever see another episode of the Kardashians again. As I approach C Town the SUV speeds ahead of me. Kim and two guys jump out of the SUV, cutting off my path. Kim yells, "Yeah bitch I saw your Facebook page and how you was talking shit about me! You're a dead black bitch for sure!" I stop and turn. The goon is up running towards me, "Shit, I'm done." But just a few feet ahead of me an old lady exits C Town with grocery cart. As I almost crash into the cart I grab it and throw it into Kim, who's running towards me. I'm enjoying this a little bit now. It's like a movie and I'm the Halle Berry character. As the cart slams into Kim knocking her and the two guys back I run into C Town dodging people who are exiting. I run through the store to the back exit that I know that leads into the projects past the garbage bins outside. I run for my life. Everything and everyone is just a blur. I run through two swinging double doors in the back where boxes and shit are piled up all over the place toward the open back door. I run. I run past two bins, over a short wall , then over a fence into the back of the projects. I run around the side of the building into an open court that leads to four different buildings. Kim and her goons are nowhere in sight. I run into one of the buildings. Thank God this front door lock as been broken for years and the city just gave up fixing it. I run through the building to the parking lot. Looks like I dodged the bullets and got some aerobic exercise. This is my luck day. On Amsterdam Ave I flag down the first empty gypsy cab and jump in the back.

"Where to Miss?"

Ten minutes later I'm at school. It's another world. Even a big public high school can seem like a haven if you've been dodging bullets on the way. I know it's easier to sit in a classroom than suffer in a basement tormented by crazy Kim's crew.

I step through the doors totally at peace with my self. "Oh fuck." The Dean is on door duty, "Jean Simon. We have to stop meeting like this." I hate when that corny bitch tries to be funny. "You're more than twelve minutes late for first period. That means that you can't join the class. Go into the auditorium. You know the drill." There's no point arguing. This woman hates me. She can also, apparently, read my mind. "I don't hate you Jean," she says before I can walk away. "I'm just trying to figure you out." She speaks as if she has a headache. "You are a bright, maybe even gifted student. When you attend class you do well, better than well, but for some twisted reason you want to play the bad girl. You know the rules. Three unexcused absences and it's automatic failure."

"I'm sorry for being late, I didn't mean to," I say in a pleading tone of voice.

"You told me the reason you quit running track was because you wanted to study boxing and judo. Are you studying boxing and judo now?"

That's sounds like a loaded question, I'm wondering why in the hell this bitch is asking me about boxing and judo. What the fuck does that got to do with anything? I'm thinking where is this crazy bitch going with this, so I say in a real soft voice, "Yeah, I'm studying judo and boxing."

"Where?"

"At a city gym right across the street from me."

"How many times a week?"

"Three days a week"

"Have you ever missed a class there?"

"Yeah a few classes, why?"

"What happened to your clothes?"

I look down and oh shit, I look more fucked up than I thought I was, but I can't tell the Dean that I've been racing bullets all morning. What can I say, that my Uncle Miles has been whipping my ass all morning, or I fell onto the train track at the subway station and the number 5 train ran me over? What in hell can I say, that shit that happened to me this morning threw me for a loop and that's why I'm late? I have a brain freeze right now. I don't know what to say. I'm busted.

"I was told you where practicing some of your judo this morning," she says in a condescending way.

"Excuse me?"

"One of the teachers from the school told me that when she was driving down 125th Street this morning she saw you putting a judo flip on a young man on the sidewalk. You almost killed him she said, he fell on the pavement so hard."

As soon as I say to her "I was not in a fight," my nose starts to bleed like I'm some kind of ghetto Pinocchio. The Dean hands me a tissue.

"I'm sorry, Jean, I'm suspending you for the rest of the semester. In two weeks when the new term begins you can return. Or you can enter the GED program. With your skills you'll have your diploma in two months and you won't have to worry about rules, which obviously challenge you."

"GED!" I'm on my way to getting an academic scholarship to college. Why are you doing this to me?" I'm thinking, does this Upper East Side bitch understand anything about how hard it is growing up in the hood? I got out of bed sick as a dog this morning just to come to school and this is the reward I get? I almost got my head blown off. What am I supposed to tell this bitch? I live in a numbers running, gambling, shot selling, reefer smoking, coke snorting house, with a crazy nigga named Miles who has both a hidden sawed off machete and shotgun under a table in the middle of the living room. I have to join a gang for protection because these young niggas out here is all fucked up and a rival gang's entire congregation is praying in unison for my death. I look at the Dean.

"Bye."

"Use this suspension time to think, Jean. Return to school, get the GED, do something productive. Don't waste your life getting in trouble and practicing judo on the streets."

THREE

Dear God,

I know that my life has spun out of my control. The guilt that I feel about Bonnie is intensified by deep, gut twisting fear now. What if the cops discover it was us? How will I protect the Street Queens? How will I protect myself? I know evil never goes unpunished and I am being punished now. I can't sleep. I am afraid of my dreams, my nightmares. To survive I have to cut myself in two. The TKO who struts the streets is as tough and cocky as ever, but the Jean who goes home every night is a trembling child. I have sinned. I am wicked. BUT I DON'T WANT TO BE CAUGHT. I'LL WAIT FOR YOUR JUSTICE, DEAR GOD. Help me escape the other kind.

Every time I get off the 6 line in the Bronx, I feel like I'm in another country. The streets teem with all kinds of Spanish mothafuckas and they are really, really loud. Preachers with bullhorns shout from all four corners, competing to save souls. From every other car that passes Spanish music blasts so loud that store windows shake. Vendors sell all kinds of crazy ass shit from their tables, including some deadly unrecognizable super fried food that looks like it'll jump up and stab your ass in the arteries if you look at it for too long. I'm just here to get my inventory from the Dominicans who sell coke and weed. There's no lock on the front door down stairs so I walk to the third floor and knock. I see an eye at the peephole. "Pape, it's me. Just open up." When he comes to the door he has a gun resting on his shoulder.

"Pape you are killing me here. The coke you sold me the last time had so much cut on it you needed to snort an ounce to get high. And the weed you sold me had enough seeds in it to grow a rain forest. I don't grow weed. I sell it. And if I want to buy baking powder I'll get it from the corner store. If you can't sell me some quality shit I will have to go somewhere else."

Pape points to Jose, a hefty young Dominican doing something with bags at the table. He cuts open one bag, revealing some beautiful fishscale coke, glistening like diamonds.

"How do you like me now? Let's say I add an extra ounce to your package to make up for last time. Will that make you happy playa?"

"Only if you come correct with the weed as well."

Carlos, another large, young Dominican walks over with his bag and lifts out a pound of weed. He hands it to me and I examine it checking for seeds and stems.

"Ok that'll work. That will work... that will keep me in business. I'll take a half pound of smoke and five ounces of coke."

Pape weighs his product and gives me my package in a paper bag. We make the usual exchange."

"Goodbye fellas. It was a pleasure doing business with you this time around."

Another day, another deal in the ghetto where money in exchange for drugs makes the underground economy go around and around. I'm female. I'm only 16 years old and I'm part of it. This is the other America and I aim to be one of its leaders. The opportunities are endless for a smart woman. I'm starting small, but I have big dreams. Someday the Jean/TKO Cartel. It's the temptation, Dear God. Church folks might say I sin. I'm weak, but when I do a job I feel so strong.

I feel so strong right now that I ignore a police car moving slowly in my direction.

I turn down the empty street between the abandon buildings as the car turns following behind me. I'm starting to breathe hard, my coat is like a smothering sauna. My palms sweat as the bag in my coat slips. If the drugs fall, do I stop and pick them up? I glance back for a quick second and notice the car is right up on my ass. I'm walking between two buildings. There's no place to run. I don't know the neighborhood well enough to find a place to hide. If this were just an ordinary time for me this shit could almost be funny. I got a crazy bitch on the loose who's looking to blow my head off. I got suspended from school, all within 30 minutes, and the Dean, who's supposed to encourage me is encouraging me to settle for a GED. And now I'm about to go to jail for drugs. It's like the old song, "If I didn't have bad luck I'd have no luck at all. "But it's not funny because this is NOT an ordinary time. It's all over the news that this morning a body was found in the river. Bloated, discolored, picked over by something, but the police believe it's the girl who disappeared on New Year's Eve. Bonnie. Fuck! Maybe I should just run and take my chances or pull out my gun and blast my way out of this, but if I'm caught with a gun I just remembered it's a mandatory two years in prison, oh shit! The car's siren shrieks loud as hell all up in my ass. I keep walking, looking for an escape. Not happening. I hear the car stop and a female voice yells "Freeze!" Fuck it, it's not my week, so I stop and slowly turn around. A young, pretty, slim, black female cop has her gun drawn on me. She orders me against the wall. I raise my hands over my head on the cold brick wall. She pats me down, finding the drugs inside the bag. She looks at the wooden door next to us and kicks it in." Get your ass in there!" I don't move and she shoves me inside. She pushes me through the empty building throwing me against the wall. She starts to pat me down again and finds the gun and says "That's another five years, but don't worry, you'll still be young when you get out of jail in 20 years."

She opens my belt buckle and unzips my pants. She puts her hands down in my panties between my legs. What the fuck is this crazy bitch doing? She starts playing with my clit with the gun to my head and I get wet. She begins finger fucking me, hitting all the right hot spots. I try not to moan and groan but can't help myself. This is some really freaky shit. This bitch is about to make me come with a gun to my head. The harder I try to fight this freaky shit the better it feel. "Fuck," I say and start coming with the gun to my head. If all cops was freaky like this, I wouldn't mind going to jail every now and again. Matter of fact, put me on the jailhouse tour. I could be freaking with police bitches in New York on Friday night and police bitches in DC on Sunday morning. I start coming a second time like mothafucka, my pussy oily wet. The cop pulls down her pants pushing me down on my knees. "Get your ass to work before I arrest your ass." I start licking her pussy that tastes like saltwater candy. She grabs the back of my head lunging my tongue deeper inside her. She comes quick and I can taste her juice in my mouth. I stand up catching my breath. We look at each other and laugh. We hug each other.

"Hey TKO, when are we going to stop meeting like this?"

The same line as the Dean, but now it doesn't sound corny. As she pulls up here pants we hear a noise at the door. Pam, my cop friend says "Let's go." I grab my drugs and gun and run with Pam. We jump into her car and speed away. She cuts on her siren and runs all the red lights. As she drives toward Manhattan, we laugh uncontrollably. When we get on the highway she slows down a little and says to me:

"You know baby, you haven't changed at all from the day I met you at my cousin Ginger's apartment two years ago when you came over to collect the numbers from her. You still have that cute baby face of yours. I wish I had your genes. Sometimes I feel I look nothing like a did last year, let alone two years ago."

"Other then gaining maybe a few extra pounds from driving around all day you look exactly the same to me. So does your cousin Ginger. She is as beautiful as ever."

"Has my hot cousin hit the number yet?"

"No, but she keeps playing, and she always asks me the same question. Do I think she will hit this week? I give her the same answer, maybe."

"You know my aunt was the same way? She never met a number she didn't like. Never hit the number once, but spent a small fortune over the years hoping, just like her mother, my Great Aunt Mary."

"I see it all the time. It's a bad habit, but it keeps Uncle Miles in fine clothes."

Pam looks at me and laughs.

"So what's up? You asked me to meet you in the Bronx. What's going on?"

"Kim from the Gun Runnin Divas gang chased me across 125th Street the other day and tried to kill me. I know she will come back to finish the job. What can you do?"

"I can't do anything until I catch her committing a crime and that still might not help you. She's is a leader of a gang, that's a small army."

"What do you think I should do?"

"You are a smart girl and you don't want to end up dead like that Jamaican girl found in the Hudson River. I suggest you find you a way out of the gang and go somewhere off to college while you're still ahead in the game."

"All that sounds simple enough, but I don't have money for college. If I had some real money I wouldn't be doing some of the thing I'm involved in now."

Pam looks at me for a moment and says, "I'm glad you called, because I have a job for you."

"What's that?"

"I moonlight as a security guard at a restaurant downtown that brings in some serious cash most nights. It's one of the last places left that's a cash business."

"How is that going to help me? And what restaurant takes cash anymore?"

"Giorgio's is easy pickings. You can help me rob the place. I don't like the stingy ass family who owns it and whatever money we take, they'll make it back within a week anyway."

"Nice rationalizing. Why are you asking me to help you? Don't you have any cop friends who can use some extra cash?"

"If I knew anyone else I could trust I wouldn't ask you. But you just told me you want cash and I think you know how to look intimidating with a gun in your hands. Also, you are smart enough to pull this off and keep your mouth shut. You have known me long enough to know you don't want to get on my wrong side. Just do exactly what I ask and there won't be a problem.

"How much money are we talking here?"

"They only make a cash deposit in the bank twice a week. I say between 15 and 20 grand, maybe more. Like I said, this will be easy. I'll take you down there and tell you how we are going to do this."

It's another school day but I'm not in school, so I have lots of time to sell drugs in the hallways of my building and go around collecting money and numbers for my crazy ass Great Uncle Miles. But there is a new problem. I collect in the very projects the Divas control. It was never an issue before because numbers are an old G thing, but now Kim's pride is hurt and I'm going have to figure out how to go inside the lion's den smelling of fresh blood without getting my brains blown out. If I tell Miles I'm afraid he'll just laugh. He thinks girl gangs are just selling wolf tickets. I'll have to become the invisible bag woman. Anyway Pam wants me to meet her on 125th Street and Lenox Avenue to take me downtown to Giorgio's so I can case the place and we can plan the best strategy for robbing it. This is going to be like the Superbowl of robberies for me. I never robbed anything of this magnitude before. I talk big, but I have never robbed anybody or anything outside of Harlem. Me and my crew have robbed Harlem bodegas, but that's more for fun than anything else, there's never real money because we stay clear of the stores that are really fronts for the big hitter drug dealers. We're crazy, but we're not stupid. Indeed this is my Superbowl and I'm going to be throwing bullets like Tom Brady throws touchdowns into the end zone. "Stick'em up, nobody move and nobody gets shot." Touch down mothafuckas, touch down…. Now where my is my trophy? And put my Superbowl ring on this mothafuckin finger right here. Now I'm going to Disney Land. Bye bye boys in the hood.

Giorgio's Ristorante impresses me. The place is huge and packed with all white people who look like they have money.

I love the big round tables with white table cloths and flowers. I see families with kids eating all happy looking and shit. And I see mothers and fathers smiling, laughing and talking all nice to their kids. And not whipping and cursing they ass out like I see in the projects. This bitch who lives right below me was cursing and whipping her two kids' asses so bad the other night that I started to cry. I'm going to have to call children protective services on this abusive ho because I can't take it anymore. I know niggas who think this shit is normal but damn. I want to ask these mothafuckas don't you get tired of cursing and beating your child at least sometimes? Maybe I'm sensitive because of my history, but if I ever live with kids I will respect them, try a little tenderness.

Pam interrupts my thoughts.

"Let's go back into the kitchen so you can make a mental picture of everything including where the bathrooms and office are. I'm going to introduce you to the son, Marcello, who counts and stashes the money in the office."

I feel nerves like a rookie playing at Giant Stadium for the first time. As we walk through the restaurant, I imagine the crowd calling out my name, "TKO, TKO." I'm looking around, but with all the noise, people, waiters and waitresses flying around all this shit looks like one big blur to me. I see now that going into the Superbowl is not going to a walk in the park. These are mothafuckin Italians this crazy police is setting up to rob. Obviously Pam hasn't seen The Godfather. If I wasn't more scared of the Gun Runnin Dives than I am of robbing this place I would run out this door back to the projects. lock myself in my bedroom and throw away the key. This is how scary this shit looks to me. In the kitchen there is an army of Mexican chefs, some so short they're standing on boxes to reach the stove. I like these little bitty men because they are about my size, half pint. But I notice there's not a black person in here except for Pam and me, not even a token Negro. You know, the kind they use in the movies for decoration. The one who gets killed off first. When I go down to see my people in South Carolina, around Monks Corner, you see black chefs and cooks everywhere, but not up here.

Again Pam shakes me out of my thoughts.

"Pay attention Jean!"

We walk over to members of Giorgio's family working side by side, making sure all the orders go out correctly. Pam introduces me as her cousin. Rosetta, Viviana, Giovanni, and Marcello, behind the counter smile, but don't stop what they're doing. Leading me to the back door Pam whispers in my ear. "This is the way to enter and exit."

This looks very doable now. I come in through the back and leave through the back instead of walking through that big ass restaurant. Inside again Pam introduces me to Giorgio himself. He looks evil, but he treats Pam with the courtesy of Marlon Brando in The Godfather on his daughter's wedding day. Handing her an envelope he says with a wide charming smile, "Happy Birthday. You know we treat our restaurant family right." I'm thinking these Italians are nice and generous. Scary as hell looking, but nice. Why does Pam want to rob somebody like him? But fuck it. I have a bounty out on me, wanted dead by any means you can blow my head off. Stab me in the back, throw me off a building, whatever. It's all good.

FOUR

Dear God,

Switchblade texted me this morning. Bonnie's parents were on NY1. They are offering a $25,000 reward for anyone who has information about their daughter's death. The police haven't called it a murder yet, but it's clear they don't think that Bonnie just wandered into the Hudson and hit her head on a rock. If my crew isn't loyal to me one of them might turn me in, ask for immunity, something like that. I'm living in an episode of Law and Order and this is no rerun. I'm afraid, Dear God, and confused and remorseful and, I feel myself spinning out of control. Nights are especially bad. My room is haunted by spirits, demons? I see Bonnie. I do. I know I don't, but Dear God, she's there. Except when I reach for her she's gone. Am I losing my mind? Should I turn myself in? Run? Can I hear Your voice, Dear God?

It's Saturday morning, and I'm still alive. I still have not told the gang about what happened with that crazy bitch Kim. I just told them when you're selling drugs downstairs, watch your back and don't let no mothafuckas run up in here and take y'all asses out. Have a nigga at the door locked and loaded at all times. Now I can try and go after that bitch like she went after me, but I'm gonna need a much bigger crew first. She's been gang bangin a whole lot longer than me and has a lot more fire power as well. I think my best bet is to do what Pam said. Lay low and stay out of harm's way until we rob the restaurant and I take the money and move down South. Today is my day to collect money and numbers for Miles. I've been doing this since I was twelve years old. I'm sixteen now and have seen a lot of things and a lot of shit people do during that time. People have told me things, shown me things, and had me doing things to them, that nobody knows about but me. I guess they think, a little girl can keep secrets. I know things about a lot of people that no one else knows. I once told my best friend about what a young former college basketball star and now a junior high school basketball coach, paid and taught me to do to him with a strap on dildo and how I grew to love it. But when I told her, she called me a liar and said stop making up stories like that on people. So I never told anyone about anything that I saw or was told ever again. I just keep it all to myself so I won't say anything about Kim right now like Pam said. Switchblade said she found another bodega we can rob soon, that's gonna be easy picking. But those bodegas never have any real money in them. By the time you split the money three ways, you only got lunch money. And if you add up the fact that everybody and their mama is selling coke and weed in Harlem these day. You get my point, I might be better off working at McDonalds. But I can't move down South with that crack head ass money. I can't go to college from money selling dime bags and robbing broke ass bodegas. I feel like

I'm between the Cross and the Switchblade, between the hell on earth and the hell below. The other thing I ask of you dear God is that you give me a kiss before dying. I'm in the dangerous month of May.

As I stroll into the grounds of the next project on my route someone calls. "TKO, TKO, child look up. Come see mama baby." Mary Jane, that crazy welfare ho is hanging out her window waving a slip of paper. "What's up? I'll see you in a second". I've been collecting money and numbers from her for the last fours years. She has never hit the number, not even once. I'm amazed at fools like her, throwing their money away. They should be putting their money in the bank, in a saving account. Try to get out the projects with all the pain and suffering that goes with it. You have to ask yourself. What's the difference between these roaches packed together in these walls and those niggas packed together in these projects, turning on each other like rats in a cage? You have to ask yourself sometimes who's the more intelligent species, us or them? Of course, that's the thing about numbers, you can play for a dollar, a dollar and a dream and the odds are better than the lottery even if the payoff is smaller. The old broken down elevator smells like Pitbull piss. The door closes and I look down at what looks like a pee lake in the corner. This must be where the roaches row their boats when they go on vacation. Before I'm even out of the elevator Mary Jane opens her door. She is still in her night gown and you can tell by the way her fro is flattened to the back of her head that she just woke up. She has three kids who are shuttled back and fourth to her mama's apartment.

She hugs me as I walk inside looking around for those bad ass kids. I don't hear or see them. They must be at grandmas thank God!

"What's been going on girl? I remember the first time you walked through that door to collect my numbers. You were a tiny little thing, but you are a big girl now with lots of money in your pocket for sure and you are looking fine as hell"

"I hear that… Where are the kids?"

"They are at my mother's this week. I need a break." Come into the bedroom for a minute where I have the money and my numbers." Mary Jane is a pretty woman. She has a caramel complexion, big dimples in her face and a perfect round mouth. Her hair is thick and bushy and her body is lean and silky. She seems to float in that brown satin nightgown she's wearing. She takes the money and the card with the numbers from the dresser and hands them to me. "Do you think I will ever hit?"

"I have a feeling this might be your lucky day."

"You think so? You really think I'm gonna hit this time?"

How the fuck do I know, but I say, "I do. I've been collecting numbers for a long time I have a feeling about these thing."

"I hope you are right. I need money bad for the kids. I'm struggling hard to make ends meet. And with this bad economy things are going from bad to worse."

"Good luck, MJ, gotta run."

"Wait a minute, baby girl. Not so fast. I have a present for you."

"What's that?"

She takes a bag of smoke from the table on the side of the bed and hands it to me.

"It's not much , but it's all I have for now and I'd like to give it to you to show you how much I admire you now you're a fine sexy looking young lady."

Suddenly her breast is in my face and her hands stroke my ass. I don't want to insult this bitch, but she's freaking me out. I know her man and I never knew her to be interested in women.

"I'm not a lady yet I don't think."

"Yes, you are and a fine, beautiful, sexy as hell one at that. I've watched you grow from a little girl into a young lady and I like what I see. I'm here and available for you anytime." She's rubbing me now. Even right now.

"Available?" I say stepping back. "What are you talking about? You have three kids and a crazy nigga you call your man."

"That's why I'm interested in you. I'm tired of that broke crazy nigga I call a man and I need me a real woman. I think that real woman is you. I need a real sister soul mate and can teach you things that only an older person could. I see the way you look at me and you know you like what you see."

Suddenly this crazy welfare bitch grabs me and kisses me in the mouth with lots of tongue and some really bad breath. With the kind of breath that you know she's been sucking dick all night without brushing her teeth. Pulling away, I look out the window.

"Oh shit!!!"

Mary Jane looks out and freaks when she sees her man Deacon holding flowers and looking up at us. I head for the front door, but Mary Jane grabs my arm."

"Wait a minute. You are not leaving me alone in this house with him are you?"

"Indeed I am. I didn't come here for all of this. I came here to collect the numbers. I'm not stupid. You really don't want me. You want my money."

Mary Jane grabs me again. Finally breaking away I open the door, but of course Deacon is standing in front of me, filling the whole door frame. Mary Jane, that conniving bitch, looks as if she is gathering her thoughts.

"Deacon, I'm sure glad to see you. I don't know what would have happened if you hadn't come."

I freak and say, "What are you talking about!" Before I can say another word the Deacon pushes me back into the living room, closing the door behind him.

"Calm down ladies. No worries. Let us all sit down at the table and talk."

"Talk about what? I'm working collecting numbers and I have to go."

"You leave when I say so. Sit down."

I feel like a prisoner on death row about to be strapped to a gurney. I can feel a dark demonic spirit following him like a shadow. If I were casting a movie about demons from hell, he would play the leading role.

"Honey, you know this is Miles' little niece TKO."

He looks at me and says "I hear you are a rough, tough, gang banger now. Is that why you are here? For some rough and tough gang banging?"

This brother makes me nervous. He's so calm, moves so slow, he sets the flowers on the table. Smiling at Mary Jane he whispers, "Honey you know what day it is, don't you?"

She shakes her head, all meek like a child. He looks at me , then her.

"It's our anniversary"

"Oh yeah."

"Are you happy?" He smiles like a wolf.

"Of course."

Looking at me, still smiling he tells her "These flower is for you dear, so go into the kitchen and get me a knife, the butcher knife."

Mary Jane and I look at each other like please don't get this nigga a knife. She reaches down for the flowers.

"Don't worry honey. I'll put the flowers away."

He pulls the flowers from her, littering the tables with petals and leaves.

"Go get me the butcher knife, please."

Because he's staring I feel my coat to make sure Jericho is there. The Deacon begins to undress me with his eyes, which reminds me how he got the name The Deacon. The story goes that in the Black church the Deacons always count the money in the basement of the church. And this crazy nigga, who probably never saw the inside doorway of a church, used to keep the drug dealers he ran under control by taking them to his basement and raping them. They said he kept empty corn oil bottles lined up around the basement as trophies of his conquests. When I came here to collect for Miles this is not what I had in mind. This nigga must love prison because prison is the biggest gay bar in the country. He looks at me rubbing his hand on his dick."

"You mind if I play the numbers?"

"I don't mind, that's what I'm here for. To collect."

He tears off a piece of paper from around the flowers and writes down his number and his name as Mary Jane creeps into the living with a large knife in her hands. She carefully hands him the knife and he hands me a twenty dollar bill and the numbers 6 6 6 written on the paper.

"Sit down Mary Jane."

I stand to leave.

"Sit back down next to Mary Jane."

I hesitate, but sit. I have to think. The Deacon rips into the wrapping of the flowers with the business end of the knife. Without looking at him I feel him staring.

"I hear you butch bitches love turning straight females out. Is that what you are here for? To turn my bitch out?"

He cuts at the paper more and more savagely. Suddenly I feel Jericho kicking me in my side and the room beginning to spin. I grab my coat, trying to get Jericho to stop. I feel myself getting dizzy, the room spinning. I see Deacon talking but I'm deaf. I can't hear anything. I just feel Jericho kicking harder and harder. I hear Jericho whispering over and over, "Let me come all over The Deacon and Mary Jane."

"Mothafucka snap out of it," I say to myself. I realize this nigga has taken his shirt off. His body has all kinds of black shank marks and shit all over it. His exaggerated steroid muscles pop out like balloons.

Mary Jane is soaking wet. I can feel her blood pressure rising. Trying to smile she tells The Deacon, "You know I would never do anything to hurt you. You know I love you. When TKO started hitting on me I didn't know what to do."

"What?" I say, thinking this bitch is pathetic.

"Yeah I was really beginning to feel violated and when she kissed me that totally through me for a loop!"

"Violated? You came on to me bitch. This is some woman you got here, Mr. Deacon."

The Deacon moves back, throwing his chair across the room. I jump up looking at the door as Deacon spins grabbing his rock hard dick bulging from his pants. He yells at the top of his lungs.

"Since you two ho bitches want to freak together I wanna watch! You gonna come in my house and fuck my bitch on the day of our anniversary? Well go ahead. I want to see you do your thing!"

He runs over and slaps the shit out of Mary Jane and throws her at me. She flies over like a bullet, knocking me to the ground. Jericho falls out of my coat and skitters across the room. Deacon comes after me looking like that crazy mothafucka Anthony Perkins in that Alfred Hitchcock movie Psycho. He stabs at me with the knife as if this was a prison yard fight. Mary Jane is screaming, running all over the place, knocking shit over. I run across the couch, and around the table trying to get to Jericho. Deacon is screaming for me like a crazy man.

"Take your clothes off bitch."

I finally grab Jericho, my hands shaking. Mary Jane screams, pleads and cries. I pop off a few rounds that miss, which of course sets him off even more. I run to the door and shoot the top lock off. I turn popping more shoots off. One of the bullets grazes Mary Jane's head. I have to stop shooting I think to myself. Even in this madhouse of a project someone will call the cops and I can't be sure it will be Pam who answers the call, but how do I keep this nigga off me? I open the front door running, hoping I can outrun that muscle bound freak. I run down the hall to the staircase The Deacon is on my heels. I run down stairs to the first floor and almost run over a mother with a baby. I run outside, still steps ahead of The Deacon, who's panting like a horse.

"I know where you live at bitch, I know where you live. You a dead bitch and that's a promise! You hear me? You a dead bitch and you ain't gonna see it comin! You hear me?

You ain't gonna see it comin. But you gonna feel it when I sneak up on you and cut your throat!"

I run down street praying Mary Jane don't hit the numbers tonight. But the way my luck has been going she will. Then she and The Deacon will to come over to collect their money. If that happens I'm jumping off the Brooklyn Bridge. I need to talk to somebody right about now. When I finally stop running I can't catch my breath. I'm coughing and my nose is bleeding. My chest feels like an elephant is sitting on it. Reverend Hamilton's brownstone is on 139th Street and thankfully I'm nearby. I'm not going there just to collect the numbers from him today. I need for him to pray for me right about now. I love Reverend Hamilton. He and his church do good things in the neighborhood. I don't know why he plays the numbers. He has plenty of cash, so I guess he plays them for old time's sake. He said once he plays because it reminds him of Harlem in the old days, when everyone played numbers for a dime or a nickel. I'm glad it's not a dime or a nickel now, because I would hate to have to count all that change. I hope he don't mind me coming to his brownstone this early. He is usually the last person that I collect from. But I really can't wait to talk to him and ask him to pray for me and to tell him I'm thinking of coming back to the church. I think maybe that's what I need, something to connect me to a real community. I don't need church for

God. I believe in God. We have a relationship. But I think I need relationships with people and whenever I pray with the Reverend I feel renewed, refreshed and at peace with myself. I said once that I have a crooked soul. Since that thing with Bonnie I feel more and more twisted. My life is nothing but one stupid incident after another and all for what? Smoking blunts at night is not helping go to sleep anymore. I'm going have to find something stronger to knock me the fuck out. God? I can't wait to tell the Reverend that I want to turn my life around but I need his help. God truly works in mysterious ways if my run in with The Deacon brought me back to Him. But that's the contrast. The Reverend is blessed. The Deacon is cursed. The Reverend has a very smart, beautiful, wife who is some kind of big shot in DC for the Obama Administration. I saw her picture in the paper just the other day with Obama and Michelle. That gives the church ladies an opportunity to care for him while the Mrs. is away. I hear all the sisters in the church love them some Reverend Hamilton who they call big old fine handsome black man. I don't even go that way. But you have to call a fine Preacher a fine Preacher when you see one. What can I say… The ladies love cooking dinner for him.

I ring the Reverend's bell and wait, but don't get a response. The first glass door is not locked and the wooden double doors in front of it are slightly open. I ring the bell again. I know he must be home because the door is open. I open the door and I hear gospel music playing in the back of the house.

"Reverend?"

I know his wife is probably working down in DC this week. I walk down the long hallway, past rooms decorated with paintings and antique furniture. The gospel music grows louder as I get closer to the end of the hall. As I approach the room I hear weird noises. It sound like niggas fucking and bitches screaming and shit. I'm wondering what the hell is happening in the Revs house. This don't sound like a preacher man's house to me.

"Good Lord, have some goddamn mercy on me!"

I step back into a corner and can't believe this day and what hell I'm bearing witness to right now. The Reverend is sitting on his brown leather couch, butt ass naked, except for his white socks and brown shoes. He's with two naked teenage boys. One kid is tonguing the Rev in the mouth, while the other kid is on his knees between Rev 's legs, sucking the Rev's dick like he's trying to get a dick sucking scholarship to college. The two flat screen TVs in the room are playing different porn films as gospel music rocks. As I turn to leave, the Rev jumps up, coming all over the boy's face. Good Lord yo, the Rev is a real freak. I guess he doesn't have time to pray for me today. I turn and the floor boards under my feet crack and groan. Or maybe I groan. The Rev looks up at me. He puts a towel around his waist trying to conceal his shame. He runs me down and turns me around.

"Jean. Please. Wait. I didn't mean for you to see that!"

"I don't care what you do. I just came over to collect the numbers."

I walk away. He grabs my shoulder, turns me around.

"Wait. Let me give you some money. Not for the numbers, but for you. Wait here. The two young freaks look back at me. They are still naked. I guess they're not finished working. These are young boys. They can probably go all day and night. They are not even trying to dress. They just look at me like I have two heads or something. I've only collected two numbers and I have no strength to finish the day. I am shocked, devastated. In my heart I always imagined the Reverend would save me when no one else could. That's one more thing I've gotten all wrong. The Rev appears with a large roll of cash.

"Now that's what I'm talking about, hush money. I can fuck with hush money religion all day, Rev."

He hears the tears and the sneer in my voice, but he hands me the money and I damn sure take it.

"I'll come back to pray and tell you about the trouble I've seen another day, Reverend," I tell him, almost choking on the words. "Now that I have the money to get me some help, I guess I'll be calling up Jack Daniels tonight."

"I'm sorry. I am sorry."

"Don't worry about it I understand. I understand you have needs also."

"Stop Jean."

I turn, but all he does is give me his numbers.

"If I hit the number I want you to have that as well and if I can ever do anything for you let me know. I'll be there."

Oh Reverend. You need more help than helping me could ever give you. The Rev started a school for boys in Kenya. Rich folks from all over the city gave money. The mayor's foundation offered matching funds. The man was a credit to his race. Shit. What the fuck is he training them to be over there? Professional dick suckers, so after graduation he can send them to out to churches around the world to suck preachers' dicks? And what do they call their high school basketball team over there, The Blowtrotters? I just hope the Rev's wife is not on the same shit down in the White House freakin with Michelle Obama.

The bitterness is running down my throat. I came to the Reverend to catch my breath and I'm choking again. This time from rage and disappointment. I'm so glad that my great grandma is not around to witness this corruption. Thank you grandma for feeding me the milk from your breast. You always knew I came out of a dead, broken womb that was immune to my cries. They wonder why we youth are bankrupted morally and spiritually. Well the whole mothafuckin society is morally and spiritually bankrupted.

Wounded as I am I am a soldier. I do my job. I collect for Miles. Exhausted, I hand Miles and Pinch the money and the numbers. Please I pray, "Don't let Mary Jane hit the numbers tonight for the first time." There are two men I never want to see again. The Reverend and The Deacon. Before I go to sleep. I tap my magical slippers three times and make a wish, that when I wake in the morning. I'm on a boat with a one way ticket to anywhere but here. But again I can't sleep. There is still no escape. When I drift off I dream about The Deacon. We are both wearing white robes, holding hands, walking towards a hellish, fiery, volcanic lake. We walk into the boiling lava and stop. He raises his right hand and prays to the devil. He baptizes me, submerging me in the boiling lava. And in the morning I wake from one nightmare into another. Pinch and Miles are standing over me wiping my face.

"What going on? Why are standing over?"

"You know who hit the numbers for the first time?" Miles asks with a smile.

"Oh shit! Mary Jane hit the numbers for the first time."

I don't wait for an answer and start to panic, pacing the room.

"No. It wasn't Mary Jane." Relieved I throw my hands up and dance across the room.

Miles says, "Guess what number hit for the first time?"

"What?"

"666," he says.

"Oh shit!" I accidentally gave Miles The Deacon's numbers. I meant to throw that shit away. I'm stunned. Life seems like it's a game organized by a cruel monster with a demented sense of humor. How bad can one's luck get? The nigga who tried killing you one day is collecting money at your house the next. Pinch looks at me and I know she's wondering what's wrong. Miles just asks, "The Deacon says he coming over here tonight to pick up his money and says that he needs to talk us both. Why would he want to talk to you? Be here a 8 o'clock. Whatever you did, I'm sure he's going to tell me all about it. I keep tellin you to slow your roll."

Why is it that every black mothafucka I know in Harlem has lost their damn mind? Doesn't Miles know that The Deacon, is the kind of mothafucka that would come over here and turn this whole house into a battleground? I decide to call Pam and ask her what to do when that crazy mothafucka comes over. We need to rob those Italians yesterday. I need to get bank, so I can get the hell out of here.

"Trust no one," Pam says. "Call the War Dogs and Street Queens and wear a bullet proof vest under your coat."

Bullet proof under a coat. I know Pam has no idea how hot these project are in the winter and how much oil the city burns heating the projects. But fuck it, it's better to be hot on earth, than dead and hot in hell.

"And honey," Pam says. "No real worries. Soon come for our little project."

I hope it's before soon come for me. That crazy shit through me off yesterday. I didn't realize that I had put The Deacon's number in the envelope last night. What did that old school song say, "If I didn't have bad luck, I wouldn't have any luck at all."

At about noon Switchblade and I head out to meet the crew, Missy Capone, Scarface Pretty, and 9-mm Rottweiler at Big Wolf's basement apartment, If you can call it an apartment. It's in an abandoned bricked up brownstone surrounded by other abandoned brownstones. The shit looks completely tore up from the outside and every window is all the bricked up, with the exception of the basement gate and metal door where you enter. Big Wolf gets his electricity from a electrical pole outside with wires buried in the sidewalk. His running water comes from a pipe in the streets. His roommates are the rats and big ass cockroaches that might self identify as something else. As we approach the basement I call Big Wolf on my cell phone to come open the gate and door for me and Switchblade. When I look at Switchblade I still see hope and song birds in her eyes, although she will be with me tonight, holding cold iron and steel. She is just like me, only a child lost in an unpromised land with bad dreams written on the walls.

Everyone else is already there, sitting around a table of weapons under a dime pig tail light in the ceiling. 9-mm Rottweiler is, as usual, talking.

"I don't know why you going through all this bullshit. Why don't you just let me and Big Wolf sit in wait and ambush this nigga? This is what I do, lay niggas down. So what's the problem?"

"I've been knowing The Deacon all my life, before he went to prison. He wasn't always this nuts. And my uncle is crazy and got a lot of juice in Harlem. Why would The Deacon do something crazy in Miles' crib?"

"If this is such a rational nigga, why did you call us?"

"He did hit the numbers and he's probably just coming for his money."

"This is a Vampire who has made a living in and out of prison, suckin the blood of other Vampires. And you wanna wait and let a nigga like that draw first blood? You got to meet him in the valley and drive a stake through his heart with a spear. Having garlic pinned to your door when he comes ah knockin' is not going to save yo soul."

"He's got a baby mama and three kids to feed and he's about to collect twelve thousand dollars. Why would he risk all that and go back to jail?"

"You sound like we are some kind of diplomats negotiating for world peace. We are overcrowded, dehumanized rats living in a world where no one gives a shit about us. You forgot where you at? This is the hood, it's kill or be killed."

"I still think we should wait and see what he wants to talk about with Miles first, before we do anything rash."

"I tell you what, you and Switchblade lay in the cut inside the crib. Me, Missy Capone, Scarface Pretty and Big Wolf will follow The Deacon inside the building. After he enters the crib we gonna wait outside at the door. And If we hear any shit that's about to go down we gonna come through that door, and start cuttin mothafuckas down!"

Everyone looks like they are itching for a fight. The only problem is it's my house and I don't need any problems in the place where I live, especially a fucking shoot out. This is not some cowboy movie where the gunfighters meet on the edge of town. This is my fucking house yo. But Miles don't want to seem to listen. Why is he letting that crazy mothafucka in the house in the first place? And why don't he want me to tell him what happened first? That's that old male nigga bullshit where they think they always must be in control no matter what. And that's the kind of bullshit that could get us all killed. I looked into that crazy nigga's eyes when he was chasing me around and there was nothing there, no heart, no soul, not nothing, only the look of... "I'm raping, sodomizing, and doing things you never heard before, killing you two bitches today." I hope I never get to see a look like that in anyone's eyes every again. From what I saw yesterday, no matter how hard, rough and tough you think you are there will always be a mothafucka, who's a whole lot crazier than you.

Eight o'clock. Switchblade and I are pacing in my bedroom, checking and rechecking our guns, waiting for The Deacon. Miles and Pinch are in the living room watching TV and eating dinner, totally oblivious to what happened yesterday. And how crazed that nut was. A normal person in that situation would have come in and told me to get the fuck out. Then confront their partner later. But not him, he came in and took it to a whole new level. It's 8:15 and no sign of Deacon. 8:30. I call Big Wolf.

"Do you see him walking down the street?"

Pinch calls, "Do you ladies want something to eat?"

"No thanks, Miss Pinch," Switchblade says.

I don't want to be eating my last supper when that nigga walks through the door. 9 o'clock. I can't believe a black mothafucka is even late picking up cash money. You know what they say, "A black mothafucka is gonna be late for their own funeral." Big Wolf calls saying they are getting tired of waiting and want to go get some Chinese food

"Stay put and don't move."

Before I can hang up Big Wolf says "Copy that. The Deacon is walking down the street with two huge goons."

It's hot as hell in here and we are wearing T shirts, bullet proof vests and a damn coat.

"Switchblade, get ready."

She looks scared. "Relax. Everything will be okay and no matter what happens, I love you."

She looks at me with a forced smile.

"Okay."

When I started both my gangs I thought we were the ones who was gonna take the war to the enemy. But it's the enemy who's coming to take the war to us, and they are a battle tested, formidable, adversary. I would rather go to war with the Gun Runnin Divas tonight than fuck with this sadistic ass killa. He's coming with two thugs for a reason and it's not good.

I hear a knock and Miles calls me. Switchblade walks with me into the living room. The Deacon's two goons are so ugly and huge that Switchblade almost passes out. I notice the two goons are identical twins with the same short Afro.

Miles smiles. "Take a seat."

The Deacon glances over at me with a look like "I'm gonna kill all you mothafuckas tonight." I look over at Switchblade who has turned completely red. There's a bottle of liquor on the table and Miles pours them a drink. They both drink it down in one gulp, staring at each the like two alpha male gorillas sizing each other up before battle. Miles pours more drinks, looking at the goons.

"I thought you came here to pick up your money, and tell me something about my niece Jean."

"That right, what I got to say is yo niece is a real disrespectful bitch. The day of my anniversary with my children's mama, this bitch came over and tried to fuck my wisdom."

"If you mean your lady what's wrong with that? She'll probably do a better job than your steroidal ass. And besides, you are in and out of prison all the time. Somebody got to fuck the bitch when you're gone."

The Deacon's black complexion starts to turn red, so do the whites of his eyes. The two goons grows a little fidgety. My stomach muscles tighten. I feel sick in my gut. The

Deacon, with a crocodile smile, says to Miles, "I'm happy you got a good sense of humor, but that's not gonna help yo niece tonight. I put it to you this way. I'm gonna whip your niece's ass tonight just like I would do a man for disrespecting like that."

"Oh really?"

This shit is beginning to sound to personal to me and I get the sense this is not about me, but some old beef between the two of them. The Deacon has come to claim his winnings and settle a score. I'm just the fuse that lit the dynamite. Miles laughs, "As you are whipping my niece's ass what am I supposed to do, sit around and watch?"

"I don't give a damn what you do, you can buy tickets to the show for all I care."

"You must have lost your mind comin' to my house like this. I can take you out seven days a week and twice on Sunday!"

"That's funny. Take me out. Take me out. Bitch you couldn't take me out if I had both hands tied behind my back."

I look at the large three by four picture on the wall next to me, of Miles' favorite old school fighter, former heavy weight champion, Sonny Liston. His hands was twice as big as the average man and ten times as powerful. I suddenly realize that not only the two goons looks exactly like Sonny

Liston, but The Deacon as well. Huge, dark skin, black tailored mustache, short Afro, and large, black, dead man penetrating eyes encased in a face sculpted from granite. Sonny Liston went to prison in the fifties for robbing white men with his fists. He learned the fight game by beating niggas down in prison.

The Deacon grows angrier. "Let me introduce you to my crew. The one to the left is the Bone Crusher, my demolition man. To the right is Bobby, my house painter. The only color he likes is the color red. And I'm the fuckin contractor!"

I look at Switchblade starting to shake. I hear something like pee hitting the floor and I look down and Switchblade is peeing in her pants all over the floor, as she whistles past the grave. We look down at the river of pee, traveling towards the table. The pee travels under and around Deacon's shoes like water under a bridge. The Deacon watches the pee travel around his shoes and smells the air like a bloodhound. He looks back at Miles.

"This is disgusting! I can't believe you came to a gunfight with two bitches in heat."

Whatever this mothafucka is planning on doing I hope it's soon. The coat and vest is so damn hot it's becoming unbearable and impossible to breath. Sweat pours from my face, hitting the floor like rain drops. I feel off balance, dizzy. The room tilts. Oh my God... oh my God. I see Sonny

Liston in the picture coming to life. He's moving and yelling, but I cant hear nothing. He's punching the glass in the frame shaking the wall. Oh God, he broke the glass, which shatters on the floor. He's climbing out the picture, oh my God, angry and cursing. Sonny Liston walks over to one of the goons and whispers in his ears. Then he moves to the other goon and whispers in his ears. He walks over to The Deacon and whispers in his ears. The Deacon gives him a gun. What the fuck? Sonny Liston with the gun is walking over to me. What the hell should I do? Jericho is screaming, "Shoot and kill everybody in the room." Sonny stops right next to me with the gun in his hand. I hear The Deacon talking to Miles.

"Listen, pay me twelve hundred to one instead of six hundred to one and I will walk out that door and all will be forgiven."

"You leaving here with only six hundred to one if you leave at all!"

I see Miles' hand on the hidden shotgun under the table. Again the room spins. Switchblade is crying. I want to hold her one last time just in case this is our last moment together. But I can't, because Sonny Liston has got a gun to my head. This is a nigga's worst nightmare, being in a gun fight with four Sonny Listons. The room spins and Jericho curses me. "Punk!!!"

Miles gives Deacon an envelope. "Here's your money fool. What time is your construction crew going to work?"

Sonny Liston cocks the trigger to his gun calling me a dead bitch. I see Miles with his hands under the table holding the shotgun in one hand and the machete in the other.

With fire and brimstone in his voice I hear Miles. "You just crossed the Rubicon mothafucka!"

The Deacon jumps up knocking the chair away as the two goons open their coats. And then, like a movie, I here... "Open up. Police!"

Deacon motions to his goons to stop. Miles tells me to open the door. On the thresh hold are a cop and a company of fire fighters. "Where is the fire?" Deacon points. "In the back." The fire fighters run to the back as Deacon and his goons rush out the door. Sonny Listen runs his ass back inside the picture frame on the wall. I walk over and huge my baby Switchblade. Think God we made it out of this alive.

Miles is pissed off. "I had my cop friend Thomas come over to put out the fire you started. I know you got kicked out of school and you think you are a big time gang banger, but you ain't no real gangsta, because all the real gangstas are dead!"

FIVE

Dear God,

I confess. It's not just guilt that's tormenting me now. It's deep, gut wrenching, fear. Out of respect Dear God, I don't use street language when I speak to you, but I'm fucking scared. I am losing my mind. I know you saw what happened with Sonny Liston, because you see everything. I didn't imagine him emerging from that picture, I saw him before me. I SAW HIM. Can I pray away my sickness? Can I pray away my fear? Can I get away, or is this the wages of sin, Dear God? Am I cursed, condemned to a life of torment even if the law never connects me to Bonnie's death?

It's been five days since The Deacon hit the numbers and tried turning my place out. I'm still alive, but I now have Kim and the Gun Runnin Divas with a bounty out on my head and The Deacon coming after me. It seems I have more enemies than friends, which is not a good look. The goons that The Deacon brought over have seen my face. You could tell by the cold blooded look in their eyes they've killed before. I'll be just another notch in their guns, another dead nigga in Harlem, that's all. Crazy Mary Jane made a stupid mistake and I've pissed the wrong nigga off. I need to find me some silver bullets in a hurry if I have any chance at all of moving down South and becoming something other than a sorry loser. Truth, I'd like to be a writer. I think my stories could help people, but I'll be lucky if I make it to next week in good health. The truth is, sometimes I wonder if the game is worth the pain.

I try to be a good leader to my gang, to give everyone an opportunity to put cash in their pockets. But a gang is not a democracy, so sometimes I have to assert myself and not give a fuck what those mothafuckas think. That's what's happening today, a little TKO assertion, or should I say insertion? I'm inserting my own special person into the War Dogs G Gang, my Hakeem, a babyfaced, sweet as pecan pie student at LaGuardia High School For The Performing Arts. He sings. He dances and he gets harassed by those stupid mothafuckas in the projects who think that anyone who wears his pants above his ass is a punk. I've been knowing Hakeem since he was a child performing in talent shows at the community center we used to have before budget cuts closed it down. He was like a young Michael Jackson, singing and grinning, moonwalking. He always brought down the house. Maybe that's what these aimless mothafuckas can't stand about him. He can actually do something. Just yesterday I had to intervene in the lobby when two wanna be gangstas pressed him against the wall, ripped off his backpack and began flinging it to each other like a frisbee. "Whacha gonna do about it faggot?" one asshole taunted him. "This mothafucka," I said, coming behind him and settling Jericho comfortably in his back. "Shit TKO. We was just messing around." But that was one day when I just happened to be there. So my plan is to put the power of Street Queens and War Dog G Gang behind him. And since Hakeem is not a punk, I made the offer as a business proposition. "Listen Babyface," I told him. "We could use you and we could help you. We need a safe place to stash our stuff, guns, drugs, whatever. And you and your mama are known as law abiding citizens here. You be our safe house and we'll make you part of War Dogs G Gang."

"You'll make me a gang banger? You know I have school and lessons and rehearsals…"

"All you have to do is hold our stuff and open your door when I ask you to. Everyone will know that you're one of us. We'll even be your body guards. So?"

"When's my initiation?"

So that's what we're doing tonight, initiating Hakeem. But this time I'll use dummy bullets. I can't risk another Bonnie incident with my baby boy Hakeem.

SIX

Dear God,

So far there's no news about anyone claiming the reward for information about Bonnie. Maybe my crew doesn't watch NY1. It's funny, Dear God. No one talks about that night. It's like for them it never happened. Or do you think that like me they just stare at the ceiling every night instead of sleeping, listening for a voice, hearing the river water lapping on the walls of the room? Will I drown too, Dear God? Am I drowning now?

Not being stupid, I like to keep up with politics, so I'm really tempted to send my Congressman my plan for balancing the national budget. Legalize drugs and tax them. So much shit is sold on the street that the deficit would be closed in no time. Of course, until I can walk into the Duane Reade of Weed and Narcotics. I'll have to visit Pepe.

As usual the street is so noisy with music, car horns, preachers and hawkers that I don't even hear the police siren.

"Get inside that building so I can strip search your sweet, young ass," Pam says as she pulls to the curb. "What up baby girl? You ready to fuck some police tonight?"

"I guess!" I saying laughing "You got them two white female police freaks coming over tonight?"

"Yes indeed. What would you like to eat tonight, some Chinese or some Italian?"

"How about both? We could have a food orgy as well." We laugh.

"So what time do you want me to come over?"

"I'll pick you up at seven"

"Okay. That's cool."

"So, killa, what happened? Who was the victim of your gang initiation the other night?"

"Hakeem."

"The one you call Pretty Boy?"

"And he is indeed pretty."

"You turning straight on me now?"

"Shit Pam. This young boy is special. Any place else they'd give him a parade. He's 13. He's in a Broadway musical. The kid is talented, disciplined, ambitious. So of course he needs protection from street thugs. They think hard work is getting out of bed before noon. The other day those fools cornered him in a stairwell threatening to fuck up his pretty face if he didn't turn out his pockets. They actually thought those Broadway producers paid him in cash. And when he didn't have any money they said they'd go find his mama."

"I see. So now you're a public safety officer. You're telling me you invited Pretty Boy Broadway to join War Dogs

G-Gang out of the goodness of your heart.? So that 15 years from now when he's making movies and wins an Oscar he'll say "I owe it all to TKO who saved my pretty ass back in the day."

"Don't laugh at me Pam. Don't you ever want to help someone? Do something good? I mean damn. You're a police officer."

"That's why I became a cop, honey. To do good. Good for me. And I expect you to do good for me too, Jean."

Shit. When Pam calls me Jean I know that I have pissed her off. She's reminding me that she's the grown up and I'm the kid she "saved" the first time she met me, when she was in the line of duty and I was busted for walking with weed.

"Listen to me Jean. You need to man up. It's going down Thursday."

"The restaurant?"

"Next Thursday the Lieutenant at the precinct is hosting a birthday party there for his son in law, another cop. It's going to be tons of cops there eating, drinking, celebrating and spending lots of cash. Giorgio's likes cash for these kinds of parties. No paper trail. No taxes. A lot of cash flows through Giorgio's. Lots of their customers have big rolls of little bills to spend and for some reason that I don't know about, they only deposit cash into the bank once a week. So there might be as much as thirty, forty, thousand dollars in cash there at closing time after the party. Thursday. Come with your game face on."

"You shittin' me? You want me to rob a place the night every other cop in the city will be there? I just walk in, tell'm, "stick'em up nobody move, nobody'll get shot. Hand over the cash. No problem."

"Relax honey. It's the perfect time. No one will expect a robbery then. And I'm security that night. Only Marcello and I will be there after the party. It's our job to stow the money in the safe. And Marcello will be so drunk by the time you walk through the back door, put a gun to his head and grab the cash he'll be on his way to passing out. The kid's a lush. Marcello loves to drink with cops. And I'll make sure his glass is always full. He's not gonna remember shit the next morning. Somebody is gonna have to tell that fool the next day that he has been robbed."

If not for Kim and the Gun Running Divas out to kill me and The Deacon planning God knows what, I wouldn't touch this with a pole twenty miles long. Pam turns on the Bob Marley song "I Shot The Sheriff" and smiles as she sings along. I worry that this bitch is right up there with The Deacon when it comes to being a sociopath. I know I've got to watch her after the robbery. She could be setting me up. After all she is the police. I learned from Miles, never trust any shadow after dark. And Pam? When I met her she seduced me really. Not just sexually, though she did turn me out. It was more that she saw my vulnerability and slid right into the empty space in my soul. She wanted to "mentor" me, she said. Show me the right way to go. I saw the movie. She was Bonnie, the smart one. She chose me to be Clyde. And it didn't take long before we were having sex in an abandoned building and she was moaning and rubbing and licking me, all the time holding her cop gun to my head. Yeah I'm a hot young freak, but even for me that's a little over the top. There is something off about this bitch. After the first few times sex with her was always master and commander and she was both, telling me "eat this pussy good or else." Or else what? What's next, both of us butt naked at the shooting range with me on my knees between her legs eating pussy as she's popping off rounds at a target?

I'm glad that Pam needs to start her shift. I need to check out my crew who should be putting in a hard day's work making an honest gangsta living selling drugs. I'm a one woman social program. I'm keeping the unemployment numbers down and contributing to the psychological welfare of the community by providing much needed therapeutic drugs. Most of the people in my community can't afford therapy, but they can afford drugs to ease their troubled minds. That's where me and my business partner come in. I know a lot of people might not believe this, but most people, including celebrities, overdose on legal drugs, not weed and coke.

About a block from my project there's a commotion. I run. People are shouting, running from my building in all directions. There's panic as an older woman runs into the street and a car skids, the driver cursing, slamming on the brakes to avoid hitting her. My heart sinks and my blood pressure rises. My crew sells on the first floor in the lobby. I hold onto my gun and drugs increasing my pace. I need to see what's happening. When you see niggas running like that it only means one thing, a grave digger is in the house and more than one wishes death on me. As I get closer a nigga who looks like Kim 's brother Snake runs past me heading for the back of a moving SUV that speeds off like a rocket down the street. I run inside the building and both 9-mm Rottweiler and Big Wolf are lying lifeless on the ground. Not far away Missy Capone, Scarface Pretty, and Switchblade, are all bleeding.

"Hakeem?" I'm on the phone in a flash. "TKO. Listen to me. Hurry your ass downstairs fast."

"Switchblade, girls, what happened?"

They start screaming something about the Gun Running Divas. Police sirens blare. I grab the girls, getting them to their feet, pushing them towards the elevator. Hakeem steps out cautiously, looking scared. "Hold the door open." I hear all kinds of cop cars coming into the block. I have to get my girls into the elevator now. Big Wolf moves on the ground, moaning. I yell "Big Wolf," and he slowly staggers up. "Pick up 9-mm!" Big Wolf grabs 9-mm off the floor as I get the girls into the elevator. I can see cops running. Big Wolf, with 9-mm over his shoulder, falls into the elevator as the cops enter the lobby. The door closes. My girls are hysterical as we head up.

"Hakeem, is your mama home?"

"She's working."

Thank God we got a hiding place. We stop on Hakeem's floor and I push every elevator button floor above us, hoping to confuse the cops who I hear running up the staircase. We run inside Hakeem's apartment and locking the door behind us. "Hakeem. Cut off the TV." I lead everyone to the back room of the small apartment, laying 9-mm Rottweiler on the floor. I quickly open his coat to see where he's been shot. Thank God he's wearing a bulletproof vest. There are two bullets lodged inside the vest. I check his pulse. It's slow, but he has one and he's still breathing. Big Wolf coughs up blood.

"It's okay," he says. "I'm alright. We both wearing bulletproof vests. He alright too."

As if to prove Wolf right, 9-mm suddenly coughs as he slowly regains consciousness. Scarface Pretty, bleeding from the head and mouth looks as if she was hit by a train, but she struggles to talk." It was the Gun Running Divas. Snake came in with a hoodie over his face and shot Big Wolf and 9-mm so fast we didn't know what hit us. Then, in a flash, Kim and her bitches ran through the door swinging their bats, beating any and everything in sight. I thought they was going to kill us all."

9-mm frantically gets up, pushing us to the side. He runs to the bathroom and we can hear him throwing up in the toilet. Suddenly there's banging on doors in the hallway. "Don't move and be quiet." A few moments later someone is banging hard on Hakeem's door. After a minute or two the banging stops, but immediately Big Wolf's very loud cell phone rings. His ringtone the fool, is an ambulance siren. Big Wolf fumbles around to find it in one of the half dozen pockets in his coat but before he can shut it off the banging at the door starts again. We hear the cops say "Open up. We need to ask a few questions. Did you see anything? You won't have any problems unless you don't respond. Then, we'll kick the door down. You got one minute to open the door or we're coming in."

"Hakeem, where can we hide?" He points to under the bed. He motions to the closet also. That's a big help I think to myself. "Hakeem, go to the door, keep it on the chain and tell them you are home alone and your mother's at work."

We hide in the closets and under the bed. I hide under the bed in Hakeem's mom's room facing the living room. I leave the door open so I can see the front door from underneath the bed. I watch Hakeem open the door. A big white cop tells him to unlock the chain. As he does three big ass white cops stomp in, not good. "How old are you son? Are your parents home?"

"My name is Hakeem officer. I'm thirteen and I'm home alone. My mother is at work. I was in my bedroom taking a nap when I heard a lot of noise and sirens downstairs. That woke me up. What happened? Did anyone get hurt? Is everything okay? I 'm really psyched you're here. I'm thinking about becoming a police officer when I grow up. And carrying a gun just like that." .

The cops laugh, patting Hakeem on the back. "We'll leave you to go back to your nap. Take it easy kid. Lock the door. Don't let anyone else in until your mother comes home.

"Okay officers." Suddenly Big Wolf's phone rings again and the cops start back inside the apartment. "Is that a siren?" Hakeem says calmly "That's my mother calling me on my cell phone. My ringtone sounds exactly like a police siren. I told you I want to be a police officer just like you."

"Go answer the phone son, you don't want to keep your mother waiting."

"Thank you officers. Can you come back tomorrow and see me again?"

"We'll try" one cop says before they exit the apartment.

Hakeem, that bad boy, is a very talented kid. He was acting his ass off, cool as a refrigerator in summer. I crawl from underneath the bed, walk up to him and start hugging and kissing this little mothafucka. For first time I think a man child has got me feeling hot. This little negro is looking real sexy to me right about now. Not only do I realize now that everyone has something to bring to the gangsta game, but I know this little mothafucka is going places. I can't wait to come back and do a little hugging and a little lovin' with this talented brother tonight. I know he's going to be a big Broadway star and a successful Hollywood actor. His eye are bright as mercury, innocent as a dove's. If I had the power to create the world anew he would be born in another time and place. I would give him a birth in a garden of flowers, not in the Harlem Hospital on 135th and Lenox. I kiss his lips one more time. They taste like rain drops. We are in a ghetto world of innocent blood. Protect this child Dear God. He is not your prodigal son. I hear my crew coming into the room. I whisper in Hakeem's ear. "I'll be back to see you later." 9-mm Rottweiler walks in first, leading the blood thirsty klan.

"Where's my shovel? Where's my cross? When can we go fuck 'em up?"

I know if I let him walk out that door now he will dig the graves of the innocent before he gets to the lost. 9-mm, on the verge of tears, barks, "I can't believe those niggas came to kill us, in our own house. Let's go to Big Wolf's basement, grab the Mac-10s and go kill everyone of those mothafuckas and fuck the neighbors if they are around and in the way. Fuck it. We'll kill them too."

"That's right," Big Wolf agrees. "Let's go do them niggas. They gonna call us the Mac Ministers when we finish with their asses."

I throw my hands up. "Calm down, calm down. We got to slow our roll right now. The only place we should be going right now is to a doctor to make sure nobody has any internal bleeding"

"The doctor?" Big Wolf shouts "You know how many police is gonna be waiting at the Harlem Hospital for niggas like us to come in so the can march us straight down to Rikers Island? I don't think so!"

"Who said anything about Harlem Hospital? I know this doctor in Harlem who's got a serious gambling problem and he owes my uncle Miles a lot of money. You niggas is going to see him. Then we'll go home, lick our wounds, call it a day."

9-mm steps up to me angry. "That's some punk ass bullshit. They are laughing at us now. We need to find their asses and wipe those smiles off their nasty faces and we need to go do that shit now. We don't need some band aid. We need some fuckin blood right about now. Are you a leader of gang bangers or the Girl Scouts?"

"Slow yo roll" I say. "Listen, I once saw this thing on TV about bees. There were these small bee less than half the size of the killer bees who were trying to find and kill them. So the killer bees would send their scouts out to find the smaller bees' nest so they all could come back and kill the small bees. The way the small bees defended themselves was when the killer scouts found their nest they would lure them deep inside. Once inside they would all attack the killer scouts so they could not return and tell the rest of the killer bees the location of the small bees. That's how the small bees survived. I think it would serve us well to take a page from that book."

"Say what?" Missy Capone asks, baffled.

"What I'm saying is we should cut the head off the snake. That way we will live to fight another day. In other words, we need to lure in either Kim or her brother Snake on the down low, like the small bees lure the killer bees, and take their ass out. That way we can strike back, but nobody will know and we can go about our business without creating more problems and drama for ourselves. They won't know what happened or who did it. We want them to think we punks and go to sleep on us. Slow yo roll. We need to figure out how to take them out on the down low."

SEVEN

Dear God,

I confess. The action with the Divas excites me. That's why I'm in the game, Dear God. I need to feel my heart banging in my chest, my blood racing through my veins. I love action, the danger. Is that it, Dear God. Am I a freak? A psychopath who only feels alive when I'm hurting someone? But that's not true either, Dear God. Because afterward I feel bad. I have a conscience, but it doesn't stop me from being crazy. Or am I crazy, someone who does what she knows is wrong, but does it anyway?

The next day I'm back collecting numbers for Miles. The Gun Runnin Divas brought a lot of heat to the building fucking up business, so we have to lay low for a minute, which means I can collect for Miles and take my sweet time. And some of my sweetest time is spent in Miss Ginger's house. Miss Ginger is a stripper and amateur wrestler, a truly bad ass black bitch six feet tall, who trains other girls to be wrestlers and strippers. Some of the girls travel with her and also work at her underground strip club in Harlem when they're not on the road. I open the door to her loft and I feel like a dick head in a pussy factory. Fine black bitches in wrestling tights are everywhere. Girls all shapes and sizes are exercising, wrestling, tumbling on mats. Wrestling gear and accessories are all over the place. Ginger is at her desk posting the schedule. All of Ginger's girls laugh about "the Schedule," but it's what makes her business work. Ginger's girls all look like ladies, even if they're ladies with muscles. Every week they're scheduled for mani, pedi, waxing and hair. Every day they take a dance class in addition to their other work outs. Every day their costumes are cleaned and their dressing rooms scrubbed, all according to the Schedule. That's why I admire Ginger. She has her shit together and she expects everyone who works for her to have their shit together too. She smiles when she sees me.

"TKO. Hi honey. I've been waiting for you. I had a dream last night that I bet on a race horse and won. I feel lucky today, TKO," Ginger tells me. "I think I'm going to play a hundred dollars on the numbers today. What do you think?"

"If you are feeling it, I say go for it. At six hundred to one that's a lot of money if you win. You can almost open a strip club downtown for that kind of money."

"Not quite, but I know what you mean" she says as she turns and motions for me to follow her. This coffee colored, high cheek boned, Pam Grier fine looking bitch is every nigga's dream. I can see her in a movie about Amazon Queen bitches buck wilding on an Island off the darkest part of Africa. Looking at this shit I must admit that I believe in the same heaven Muslims believe in, a heaven that awaits you with 72 sixteen year old virgins when you die. Show me a man who don't want to see 72 virgins in heaven and I'll show you a lair. If niggas and dike bitches knew for sure 72 virgins awaited them in heaven you would have to bring Dr. Jack Kevorkian back from the dead to open up suicide missions, there would be so people wanting to kill themselves. And don't let all that moral bullshit the so called Religious Right are talking fool you. They are selling more pornography in the so called conservative family values states than anywhere else in the country. Even Malcolm X said the reason he left the Nation of Islam was because he discovered the Nation's spiritual leader, Elijah Muhammad, had fathered six children by six different sixteen year old virgins when he was over sixty five years old. Go ahead on great grand daddy. I'm not mad at you. I guess he couldn't wait to die and go to heaven to get him a taste of 72 sixteen year old virgins. He had to get his on earth, that's what I'm talking about.

But just as I was really amusing myself with this virgin shit I looked at Ginger's desk. Right there is a photograph of herself and Snake. "Ginger, is that you and Snake there together? Do you know him?"

"Yeah I know him, he just invested some money in my underground strip club. He's there all the time. You know brothers like him are hounds like in capitol DOG. Why are you interested?"

"No reason" I say, thinking, "We got this nigga now." But I like Ginger and I don't want to fuck her thing up by wetting that nigga up anywhere near her spot. I'm going to have to think of a way to catch that nigga in the valley of the shadow of death.

"What do you think about that dream baby girl?"

"I think it's good. I had a dream last week that I found money on the street and the next day I found sixty dollars. People were just walking right past it and there it was waiting for me. Dreams are good sometimes. If you don't go for it you'll never know."

"OK then. Call me when I hit the number tonight ," she says smiling. "Wish me luck."

"Good luck Ginger. Pin their asses to the mat tonight. And keep dreaming about winning," I say as I head toward the door. But I don't want to leave. In the middle of the loft girls are practicing their pole dancing, swinging and twirling on the way to the ceiling. I don't know what Malcolms X's problem was with Elijah Muhammad. I'm not mad at him. If I could turn back the hand's of time I would say to Malcolm "Life is like a photograph. You have to develop the negative before you get to the positive. Not that I see much positive here. Ginger's street depresses me. I see the same niggas on the same corners I saw ten years ago when I was a child. You have annoying niggas like these on every corner, in every ghetto in American. These ghettos are like the Barnum and Bailey Circus. The only thing that changes is the clowns.

I have so much collecting to do today because my Uncle Miles and Pinch his silent partner, is the last of the great Harlem number runners and bankers. In another ten years the numbers game in Harlem will be gone, along with the worst elements in the hood. I hope there will be more quality people coming, both black and white. There might be a new day dawning. These ghettos don't work and will never work. I heard Donald Trump is trying buy up all the projects. He can have them. I'm ready to go. There are airplanes, buses and cars. Why in the hell would a mothafucka stay in one place all her life? I know of people being born, raised and dying in the project. What the fuck are we in, that TV show The Twilight Zone?

As I give Miles the numbers and the money I've been collecting all day I take a moment to think good thoughts for Ginger. I really hope she hits the jackpot tonight, she deserves it. She works hard and is always helping other sisters find jobs and get ahead, unlike that bitch Kim, who's not trying to help me get ahead, but is trying to blow my head off.

That's the only kind of head she's interested in, a nigga's head used as a bowling ball.

An hour later my crew and I are sitting in Big Wolf's basement talking about how we can catch a black mamba and feed his body to the sharks. Big Wolf and 9-mm pace the floor. Big Wolf is angry.

"Fuck Ginger's underground strip club. I say we run up on that nigga as he is walks inside and wet his ass up like he tried to do us. This nigga didn't give a shit and wait until we was conveniently in place to shoot. They walked in and handled their business. Now it our turn to do the same."

Scarface Pretty jumps up from the couch. "Wolf is right. They walked into a building full of people and started spraying bullets as if they were Raid and we was the roaches."

"And those exterminators sprayed me first, like I was the king roach who all the other roaches needed to see die first, in order to put the fear of God in them," said 9-mm, still thinking about the moment when Snake shot him in the chest.

Missy Capone agrees. "Yeah man. Kim and her Divas didn't give a shit. Matter of fact, when she was beating my ass with a baseball bat she claimed she almost killed yo' ass a few weeks ago TKO. Is that true? Did she try to kill you and you didn't tell us, just left us standing down there selling drugs for you, exposed like that? You knew that bitch was coming back for you? Cause that's what she said, she was coming back for you."

"That bitch is lying on me. She didn't try and do shit! I say, knowing I fucked up. Missy Capone jumps in my face. "If she's lying, how did you get that knot on your head and that busted lip a few weeks ago? Did the boogie man knock your ass out? Or were you working construction and did you fall off a fuckin ladder? Which one was it bitch? Because I don't want no punk ass bitch around me!"

I'm stunned for a moment. I'm the leader of the Street Queens and this bitch just called me out. I have to think of something fast because I can lose these niggas and never get them back. So I grab Jericho and go to pistol whipping Missy Capone. I'm beating the shit out of her hoping someone grabs me, because if I stop on my own they might take that for weakness. Instead of them separating us I hear these stupid mothafuckas betting among themselves whether or not I'm going to beat her to death. Wonderful. We came here to plan how to get rid of Snake and these fools are making bets to kill Missy. "God help us…" I say to myself. Stop the madness now. I don't give a shit anymore what these damn fools think. I'm thinking I need to get rid of these niggas and find me some with some brains because these fools are like the Tin Man in the Wizard of Oz. I stop, turn and smack 9-

mm in the face because he's laughing. I shove Jericho in Big Wolf's face and yell for him to, "Shut the fuck up. I should shoot all you stupid mothafuckas in the face. We came here to get rid of Snake and you stupid mothafuckas is making bets. Niggas grow up! Now pick Missy up off the floor and lay her of the couch and Wolf go get your First Aid kit, you big dumb stupid mothafucka!"

The rest of the crew lays Missy on the couch. I feel guilty and really fucked now. Not only did I have to give a beat down to one of my most loyal soldiers, I lied and got my crew caught out there unnecessarily. I feel like crying now and saying that I'm sorry, but I can't. I'm the leader of a wolf pack, so I curse the tears away and grab the First Aid kit away from Wolf as he approaches. Scarface hands me bowl of warm water and a towel. As I wash the blood from Missy's face I see the pain and hurt in her eyes. As I wash the tears from her face I think that although we have a black President in the White House, life has not changed for youth in the ghetto. All the country's resources are still going to the banks and the military. How is fighting wars in the Middle East going to help people like us? How is that going to get us out the projects and the killing fields of America? Just as many of us are dying in a 200 mile radius of the White House as in Afghanistan and the ones who are not dead are suffering from post traumatic stress syndrome. We are suffocating in the quiet desperation we all live with but try to ignore.

I finish cleaning Missy's wounds but have nowhere to put the First Aid kit, because the table is littered with Mac 10s. Switchblade grabs a Mac 10 and says, "We are all frustrated now, fighting among ourselves. I think we all need a little taste of blood tonight. I know that's what we need to feel a little better. So why don't we just go and find all those Diva bitches tonight and let it all hang out?"

I agree. I am ready to take this shit to the limits myself. We are all probably going to die young anyway. None of us has a real future. We live with a government that doesn't even give a shit about the white middle class any longer, so what's the hope for us?

We already committed a crime and that crime was being born. "Fuck it" I say.

"Grab your weapons, killas. It's time to go hunting for that sacrificial lamb. Grab extra clips of ammo. We gonna kill more niggas than the klan tonight."

Missy slowly stands, slowly walks and slowly picks up a Mac. She looks at me and the looks says that she will be okay. I look at my crew and smile.

"Lock and load. Lets go. Time to kill."

But as we head out someone bangs on the door.

"Don't move. Big Wolf, Look through the hole in the brick to see who the fuck it is." He removes a wine cork from the peephole.

"Shit. It's Hakeem and a young girl."

"Let them in."

Hakeem, who made me get in touch with feelings I didn't know I had, walks through the door with a vision, an innocent as a dove looking, biracial, red headed babe. The redbone is slim even dressed in white. A white baseball cap hangs over her eyes. "Hakeem." The whole crew gives him much love. All these bad ass gang bangers put down their weapons to do high fives. Babyboy got a lot of heart, and we all know it. Everybody brings something to the gangsta game and he brings loyalty, a baby face even cops love and now this red angel dressed like a dove into the lions' den.

Big Wolf mutters, "Come back later we got to go."

"Just stop and slow your roll for a minute," I tell them, because I know Hakeem delivered the red fox here to join the gang, and I also see that she would be perfect bait to lure Snake, so I say, "Lets wait a minute. Obviously Hakeem brought this sister soldier here to join the gang. We can use her to get to Snake. Nobody knows her. She can get right up on this nigga and bang."

"You wait a minute I can't kill anybody. I'm half Jewish," Red says and we all laugh, breaking the tension in the room.

"Well I'm half and half my damn self," I say. "I'm Cherokee and black and that never stopped me from killing anybody. And besides why are you here if you can't kill anybody? Why do you want to join the Street Queens?"

"Excitement. To piss off my parents. To see if I can do it, new guys."

"This ain't JDate honey," I remind her.

What's your name?"

"Tracy English."

"Tracy English. We can call you Foxy Red. That okay Tracy English?"

"Cool. I like that. That's really cool. Foxy Red."

"So, when did you want to join?'

"Right now"

"That's bullshit. Right now we got shit to do," barks 9-mm.

"Come on man. Slow your roll," I tell him again. "Haven't you heard the Bob Marley Song? 'He who fights and run away live to fight another day.' Calm the fuck down nigga. Have you every thought those niggas might be smarter than us? They didn't reach the glory days of gang bangin by being fools. When David went up against Goliath he chose his first shot well. Now the opportunity for us to get rid of Snake first and then his sister Kim just walked through the door. We do this shit right, we cut off the head of the Gun Runnin Divas without all that drama."

I glance over at Foxy Red. Her arms are folded and she's impatiently tapping the floor, looking slightly bored. So I ask, "Where do you live? What do your parents do?"

My crew looks at me like "What the fuck?" Is this a sorority interview? What do your parents do? Parents? Some of us live with our moms. Some with our grandmamas. I live with my uncle. No one has parents, as in two of them. But I know my customer.

"Both my parents are consultants for the Republican Party. They're lawyers. We live on the Upper East Side. But don't think I'm one of those rich private school girls. I go to a public high school like you guys, Stuyvesant, downtown."

Now I'm thinking this is great. This is what I have been looking for, more brains in this organization. This bitch is from the best public high school in the nation, where all the best and the brightest kids in the city go if they can pass the admission exam. Also, I believe I have the finest pussy that money can buy standing directly in front of me. Oh my Lord, you got to be looking after me. I've gone from pistol whipping, ready to kill somebody, to this, all in five minutes. Good God, you are looking after me after all, cause that's some of your work, a bitch like this walking through the door. This bitch have a funky, sweet, pussy smell so strong that the aroma is screaming out of her pants.

She looks at me and says. "I don't have all night, I have home work to do and school in the morning. So where is the Old Rugged Cross?"

I look over at Big Wolf who shakes his head okay.

"Give her the Old Rugged Cross. Fuck it. I'll get the flash light and the cross and we can do it in the basement next door."

Big Wolf, moving his old, dirty, bum refrigerator out of the way unlocks a small steel door that leads to the abandoned building. The dark basement, crowded with discarded furniture and bits and pieces of things no one could recognize looks like something out of a hellish horror movie. I want to hurry up and do this and get the hell outta here because I think I see a ghost already down in this mothafucka. Hakeem looks terrified. I can't say that I blame him. Switchblade and Scarface Pretty put the cross on Foxy Red and I take out Jericho, nervous as hell about shooting this pretty red bitch. I would have preferred just to let her join, without all this gun and cross bullshit. A bitch like this would be a terrible thing to waste. If I had known she was coming I would have gotten some rubber bullets. I can't afford to lose any more soldiers, especially a pretty red bitch with some brains. This red bitch got some heart as well. She came here to a basement full stupid mothafuckas and is about to put on The Old Ragged Cross. I know grown ass men who don't have that kind of heart.

"Can you speed this up a little? I have home work to do. Can you just shoot please?"

"No problem baby. I got your back," I say to her, pointing Jericho at her chest. I feel Jericho's anger, because I didn't let him get his nut off tonight. He feels like a hot cast iron frying pan in my hands. I wanna holler but can't. I wanna scream, but refuse. I feel blinded, but can see. I feel lost because this life found me.

I pull the trigger and Foxy Red rises off the ground like a feather in the wind. Suddenly Hakeem screams, scaring the shit out of everyone. Has a bullet bounced off the vest and hit him? Jesus, worse! Two big ass rats are running over Hakeem, chasing each other. So I say to myself, thank God those big mothafuckas jumped on him instead of me. These rats down here never see people, so maybe they think Hakeem is part of the dirty furniture. Scarface Pretty screams too, pointing to the door where an army of rats is flooding into the basement. I yell for Big Wolf and 9-mm to grab Foxy Red. The two rats on Hakeem run down his arm and jump on Big Wolf. Cursing, he drops the flashlight, breaking the bulb and leaving us in complete darkness as the rats scurry over and around the junk and us. I feel the panic run through the gang as they realize that we are trapped in a rats' den. God, if you are trying to tell me something I get the message. I should quit my day job and especially the night one too.

And the room spins. I have nightmares in the dark. "God please, why are you doing this to me?" I hear Switchblade and Missy Capone scream and yell." They're biting, they're biting me!" I hear 9-mm hollering "I can't see shit," but me, I can see clearly, like it is day. I can see that man again, pointing at me. Oh my God he's riding on a giant angry thousand pound rat. I can see the giant rat is pregnant and monster babies are fighting each other inside her stomach. Oh no, the giant rat is almost on us. Everybody is screaming and praying. The giant rat runs to Hakeem, biting off his head. Oh my God. He's eating his head. I hear Hakeem 's moans from inside the rat's mouth. I can smell the rat's stink breath. And now a giant rat comes towards me, smiling. I aim Jericho and unload, shooting the rat in the head. The gun smoke smell freshens up the room. Everyone is screaming "Stop shooting, stop shooting!" but I fire until Jericho can't come no more. I hear niggas running in the dark in all directions and I start running too. Someone runs over me knocking me backwards to the ground. I fall on a huge nest of rats. Their claws scratch at my chest, my legs, my eyes. I can't breathe, hear or see, I only feel the rats gnawing my life away. I'm entombed now in a matchbook size impenetrable black steel cage. I fade away. Everything is completely black now and I'm gone.

I wake with a pounding headache. I am on Big Wolf's couch. Everyone is there except Foxy Red and my baby Hakeem. I jump up. "Where are they?" They all look at me, not saying a word. "Oh shit, not again," I say to myself as my heart begins to sink.

"What the fuck?" Like I said before, a gangsta is a terrible thing to waste. I'm getting angry now. "Where the fuck are Hakeem and Foxy Red?" 9-mm glances around the room.

"They're fine, they went home already, but they're not the ones we're worried about. It's you we worried about. Once the flashlight went out you went nuts. You started talking crazy, acting crazy, then began shooting, almost killing everybody in the room. Now I know all those fucking rats started coming from everywhere and jumping on everybody and freaked us all out, especially in the dark and all. But you took that shit to a whole new level. Hell, you are worried about Red and Hakeem, but they are ones who went back down for you, using the lights from their cell phones to find you. Because none of us here was dumb enough to go back for you, for fear you might start shooting again. And if we did go back to get you and you started shooting what was we suppose to do, start shooting back? Then we would be acting just as crazy as you."

I've known since I was a child, after my great grandmama died and I had to go live with my mother, I started coming apart at the hinges, especially when I was under tremendous stress. But 9-mm was right, almost killing my own soldiers was taking it to a new level. I knew at the moment I needed some help. But I didn't know where to go and who to ask. In the hood the only therapist we got is the drug dealer and the medications he prescribes for psychosis are weed, coke, crack, heroin, and all kinds of pills and shit. I'm afraid if I start doing hardcore drugs my hallucinations will get worse. I can't go to the hoods' therapist. He's dressed to kill, not to mention I'm a hood therapist myself. I'm a bona fide Dr. Strangelove myself, with a medical degree from the houses of pain. But fuck all that. We all got problems. I just have to learn how to use mine to my advantage, so I say with venom in my voice, "Now that y'all know I'm a crazy ass mothfucka don't fuck up and you won't get shot. I'll see you bitches tomorrow night. We are going after Snake. I'll let you know the game plan in the morning."

EIGHT

Dear God,

Am I doing wrong again? Should I have sent Hakeem and Tracy on their way? Should I have confided in them that there's nothing glamorous or exciting about this stupid gang banging life? That it's not about anything. Those kids have choices. I should learn from them. Do I still have choices, Dear God? I'm afraid that I don't. I'm afraid that the voices in my head are getting louder, more demanding, more frequent. I'm afraid, Dear God. I'm always afraid.

As I make my morning rounds I think about how to get rid of Snake tonight. I don't want to cause a scene in front of Ginger's strip club, but the Divas have come after us twice, so obviously they're not stopping until they've finished what they started. Fuck it. A gangsta gotta do what a gangsta gotta do. If we give them niggas another chance I'll be telling this story from a graveyard somewhere and that ain't happening. I don't see no difference between the animals on the Discover Channel and the ones out here in the street. A gorilla is a gorilla is a gorilla I don't give a shit where he's from.

My special stop today is Professor Michael Weeks, who's a black cowboy and Black History Professor at City College. I always enjoy collecting numbers from the Professor because I always learn something new about black history, which the Professor says is American history.

As usual, the Professor opens the door wearing a cowboy hat, vest, belt with a big round cowboy buckle and shiny cowboy boots, smelling like shaving cream. When I first met him I thought he was into some gay shit, some faggots dress up like that, but it's his lecture costume. He lectures all over the Tristate about black cowboys.

"Hello, come on in" he says with that huge smile of his.

In the middle of the room there's a long table with a lot of papers, maps, and really old looking black and white photographs of black people from a long time ago. Some folks are on horses, some digging for gold with Chinese people, some black cowboys with big ass guns in holsters, are drinking with white men in cowboy saloons.

"What are you working on?"

"I'm writing a book about the African American role in the Western expansion of the US. Our contribution to that expansion has been deleted from history. A lot of black people went West to escape to slavery. Others went as free men and women seeking better lives. Blacks in the West established some of the first black newspapers, like this one, Clarion of Freedom, started in Ohio in 1850."

This is why I like coming here. Professor Weeks is so excited about his work he gets me interested. It doesn't occur to him that a teenage number runner isn't someone worth talking to. He shows me an old photograph of a group of people, mostly black.

"These are the founders of Los Angeles, California. He shows me another photo of a man named Manuel Victoria, a career soldier and one of the first governors of California, a black man. He says black people played a major role in California's statehood. Who knew? Professor Weeks likes educating me. He says that African Americans played a major role in every aspect of the Western frontier. They were traders, trappers, miners, artists, writers, politicians, lawyers, stagecoach drivers, lawmen, outlaws, soldiers, cooks, blacksmiths, horsemen, marksmen, distillers, Indian language specialists, you name it, we did it. He showed me photographs of people like Edmonia Lewis, a well known sculptor, William Owen Bush, a wealthy cattleman whose settlement of Puget Sound, Oregon, was responsible for America's successful claim to that territory from the British, the Rufus gang who's criminal career started when they shot and killed John Barret, a black deputy marshal, Martha Williams, who disguised herself as William Cathy and became a private in the U. S. Army. and Mrs. Biddy Mason, an ex-slave who gave both land and money to build schools, churches and nursing homes. Then I noticed a photo of two men, a black man Professor Weeks said was a famous real cowboy named Bill Peckett and a white man who was a famous actor, Will Rogers. The Professor told me that Billy Peckett taught Will Rogers how to play a cowboy in the movies. Now ain't that a bitch? The white man learning how to be cowboy in the movies from brothers? That's why I love collecting numbers from the Professor. I learn new shit every time I come here. The way my school history tells it the only thing black people ever did was pick cotton. Professor Weeks said that a black male also founded Oklahoma City and he showed me a photograph of one of the first black men to hold a major political office, Edwin P. Macabe who he said also tried to make Oklahoma a black state. Now you know white people are not going to go for that, but that's still some gangsta ass shit, trying to make a black state. You got niggas now a days who can't make their way out of prison, let alone create a black state. He also said that some of the most educated people on the frontier were black females. Now I'm thinking, how in the hell did we go from some of the most educated, to three different baby daddy bitches, one nigga in prison, one nigga dead and one nigga on the run? Somebody help me Jesus!

When the professor hands me the money and his numbers he says, "Look I've been playing numbers for years and as long as I've been playing the numbers I've only hit ten times."

"Well that's pretty good. I know people who have never hit the numbers. And I also know a few people who hit the numbers the first time they played. You hit the numbers like that you should be playing lotto too."

"I like the numbers tradition. It connects me to folks who lived here when Harlem was the black capitol of America. I play to be part of that history. I really don't even think about winning."

If all of Miles' customers felt that way he might not have to pay out all the time. Maybe the Professor wouldn't notice even if he did win.

In the corner of his living room I notice that the Professor has a pile of coiled ropes.

"What's that?"

"That's rope lasso, which is designed to be thrown around a target and tightened when pulled. It's one of the tools of the cowboy trade."

"I like that," I say. "Do you mind if a borrow a few of those lasso ropes so I can take them to school and show my class?"

"Take it. Keep it. It's yours."

"Thanks professor" I say, grabbing the rope. I hug him and walk out the door.

Street Queens

Friday night in Harlem and you can feel the natives getting restless. There is an army of young niggas out here tonight with no jobs, no money, and little hope, walking the streets looking for trouble and victims. These are the mothafuckas that time forgot, but not the criminal justice system, illegal aliens in their own country, the border line the color of their skins, bastard babies in their mamas' arms, whose fathers deposited all of their investments inside the Sperm Bank Of America. This is just another night and another country, up here in Harlem, whose landlords dwell in luxury apartments down town, wealthy from their plantations uptown, deep South of the Canadian border. There's something rotten in the cotton. These young hood niggas are like characters on a stage, unwittingly playing the leading roles in a Hip Hop Shakespearian tragedy. The only difference is that this play won't be performed except on the 6 o' clock news.

My crew and I are sitting in 9-mm's uncle's beat up van with black tinted windows. We are across the street from Ginger's underground strip club, waiting for Snake to arrive. It's all kind of broke mothafuckas going in and out of the club, including old gees who get their dicks sucked for money in dark rooms downstairs inside the basement. Foxy Red is sitting up front in the van next to me. I got her dressed like a hood ho.

"Oh shit that's Snake over there with the red baseball cap and black leather jacket."

"I don't know why we are doing all this bullshit" grumbles Wolf. "Let me run over there with the ski mask on and blast that nigga. They won't close Ginger's place down just because another nigga got shot."

I tell Big Wolf to shut the fuck up, so I can explain the game plan. I glance around.

"Before we let Foxy Red go inside the club let's wait for him to get a couple of drinks in him and a lap dance. We want this nigga high and his dick on a hard before we send Foxy in there. Red, when you go inside walk straight up to him and start giving him a dick massage. Tell him to order both of you double shots of the strongest drinks they got. Then order more drinks until that nigga is higher than Old Dirty Bastard was the night he died. Tell him you want to take him home to fuck the shit out of him. When you leave, put his ass in the cab and drive him to the basement. That way when he disappears, no one will know what happened to him or which niggas did it. The only thing people will realize is that when he left the strip club he was already a ghost."

Everything seems fine. We send Foxy Red into the club and about an hour later we a leave 9-mm in the van and go back to the basement with enough time to set up the electric chair in the living room. I also set out two dozen glass candles around the room. This shit is looking real medieval. Then the phone rings. Foxy Red and Snake have just jumped into a gypsy cab.

"Switchblade, Missy Capone, Scarface Pretty, Big Wolf. Get ready. The black mamba is on it's way." We disappear and wait, but not long. We hear Snake.

"I hope you don't live here, because this place looks like some kind of S and M joint. Are you some kind of dominatrix or something? Because if you are I'm more than willing and able to get into some shit like that tonight. I'm ready. Tie me up and kick my ass. I'm ready for that kind of freaky shit tonight."

I love a nigga like this, a willing victim. Snake sees the Cognac and glasses on the table. "Drink?"

Red pours and starts removing his clothes, but he gets a call and the dick answers. In a minute he clicks off, but something isn't right He's pacing, distracted. Foxy Red wraps her arms around his neck and her legs around his body. She lightly licks his ear, his mouth, trying to get him to relax again, but he looks hyped up, so she strips, slowly, caressing herself as she takes on and off her tiny top, her thong. She moves toward him, puts one breast in his mouth withdraws, smiles. Snake smiles back and grabs her, so she pushes him into that chair in the middle of the room. The electric chair. Now Red sits down on him, unbuttoning his shirt, licking his nipples, whispering something that makes his pants bulge so tight that he almost bursts his zipper, but she reaches down and releases Snake's snake. He's wild, pulling down his pants, groaning. He tries fucking her, but she pulls away, unwrapping a condom and rolling it carefully, slowly down his hard dick. He's almost out of control, bucking and groaning, screaming "I'm gonna fuck you to death bitch. I'm gonna slam this snake right through you."

"Now!"

Switchblade, Missy Capone, Scarface Pretty and I are there and before he can finish the lasso ropes are around him. He jumps, throwing Foxy Red to the floor.

"What kind of S and M, dominatrix shit is this?'

I yell back, "The Street Queens kind mothafucka!"

We tighten the lassos around his neck, struggling to pull him in four directions. But he is fighting, kicking, punching the air trying to break free. Out of the corner of my eye I see 9-mm, but Big Wolf holds him back laughing.

"Let them bitches do this by themselves since they didn't want me to blast his ass. Fuck'em. Let them bitches fight with that nigga."

Snake's face turns from black to red, his eyes seem to pop out of his head. He's biting off his own tongue. We just should have shot this nigga. I need go smoke me a mountain of blunts and watch reruns of the Kardashians all night after this shit. I need to call little Hakeem to see if he wants to come upstairs and ask if he wants to eat some pussy and fuck the shit out of me tonight because, I'm gonna need some dick for the first time after this. We have been trying to choke Snake for almost five minutes and he is still fighting. What the fuck was I thinking when I decided to get medieval on this mothafucka?

"Please, somebody shoot this freak!"

Foxy Red grabs a gun and fires at Snake and almost blows my head off.

"Bitch stop shooting!"

Snake breaks loose and runs up on me. I can't breathe. He's strangling me. Big Wolf has stopped laughing now. He pauses to shoot, but Snake turns and grabs the gun. As he and Wolf struggle 9-mm runs over to help and Snake points at him, shooting, as Wolf grabs for the gun. It's a dog fight up in this bitch and Snake is winning. Snake slams Big Wolf to the floor knocking him out. Oh shit, Snake has the gun. He stumbles around trying to shake the cob webs out his head. I get to my feet as he points the gun at Switchblade, who's running around the room, trying to find cover. He fires and misses, then aims at Missy Capone. I get up and Snake has us all running around the basement trying to shield ourselves and one another. Wolf and 9-mm were right. We should have killed this nigga as soon as he stepped in front of the club because now he's gonna kill us all in this fucking basement if we don't get out of here now. Finally Big Wolf throws the refrigerator aside and we find the small door to the abandoned building, willing to take our chances with the rats. I see Snake staggering into the kitchen, shooting in our direction, but Big Wolf runs up and grabs Snake from behind as 9-mm grabs a knife from the kitchen. He runs over to Snake who kicks him so hard he rockets backwards towards us. He falls into us almost stabbing Missy with the knife. 9-mm yells, "Come help kill this nigga." He runs back over to Snake as Wolf tries to throw Snake to the ground. Now it's two Rottweilers against one powerful black mamba in a gun and knife fight. 9-mm stabs at Snake as Big Wolf holds him, but Snake is true to his name, slithery and flexible, so he twists away from them. Finally 9-mm kicks Snake in the chest as hard as he can. 9-mm falls backward onto Big Wolf, but gets back to his feet and this time stabs Snake in the chest. It's a blood bath.

Big Wolf staggers over to me coughing out his words, "I told you to shoot his ass tonight."

Suddenly loud police sirens scream down the street.

Big Wolf yells, "Put on all the chains. Lock the iron gate outside, then lock the double steel door."

Foxy Red, still butt naked runs into the living room for her clothes."

"What are we gonna do with the body if the police come here?" Missy Capone moans.

"What do you think we gonna do with the body if the police come here? We're gonna have the body waiting for them in the living room. Then we going tell them, first we tried to strangle him, then when that didn't work we tried to shoot him and when that didn't happen, we stabbed him to death. That's what we gonna do, you silly bitch!"

I look at Wolf, "Big Wolf, come with me to the roof so we can see what's going on. If the police try to come in here escape through the abandoned building next door."

Big Wolf grabs two flashlights this time and we head up to the roof. "Be careful," Big Wolf whispers. "Watch where you're stepping because it's weak and you can easily fall through."

For some reason black smoke is everywhere. I take one step and my left foot immediately goes through the roof.

"Big Wolf!"

He pulls me out of the hole and we gingerly walk to the edge of the roof. Leaning on our stomachs, looking down to the street, we can see a raging fire in a brownstone. There are fire trucks and a crowd of people watching the fire fighters working to get the blaze under control. Big Wolf looks a me and whispers.

"We got to get that nigga out of my house tonight before the body starts attracting the rats. I'm talking tonight. I told you to let me hit that nigga on the street. That chicken shit didn't work so now there's fuckin blood everywhere. That's a problem yo."

"Let's get rid of the body now," I say.

"Now? Don't you see all those fuckin cops and firemen and muthafuckas down there. Bitch are you crazy?"

"No man. This is the best time to do it. No one is gonna notice we're carrying a body out with all that shit going on in the streets."

Anyway, I can't wait to get off this roof. It feels like the whole thing is going to fall through. 9-mm is waiting for us in Big Wolf's apartment.

"Get the van," I tell him. "We are going to wrap Snake in trash bags and get him out of the neighborhood that way."

9-mm looks at me for a moment like I'm crazy , but he goes.

"Foxy Red. Go with 9 mm and hide in the van. Ya'll be too conspicuous going out with us. Big Wolf, grab the clear plastic and large green garbage bags and whatever sheets and towels you have. We wanna prevent any blood from dripping."

I have to give it to the brother Snake. He fought like mothafucka for his life. For a minute I thought he was going to kill us all. I do feel bad for Foxy Red. She saw the gun in the nigga's hands. I felt her terror, butt naked, screaming. That's a tougher initiation to Street Queens than any of these other gang bangers had. I don't expect to see her again after tonight. And if I do, she's a bigger fool than I think. I'm the leader of the gang and I want to get out of this shit myself after tonight. Niggas like Snake, you have to shoot with silver bullets, then drive stakes through their heart in order to kill them.

Packaging the body isn't easy. I act like I know how to do it, but I'm making it up from movies I've seen. First, I make everyone take off their clothes so they don't soak in Snake's blood. Then we duck tape plastic around the body and carefully lift and drag it, easing it into more bags.

"Check yourself for blood stains everyone. Look at your feet for splatter, your arms, your eyebrows. Scarface Pretty and Switchblade, make sure all the candles are out."

My phone rings. It's 9-mm saying there's cops and people everywhere because of the fire.

"Good for us. No one will notice when we carry the body out, especially because we made it look like more trash."

Outside Missy Capone puts the chains and locks on the gate. "Oh Shit." Three white cops step from out of nowhere.

One asks, "'You guys doing demo this time of night?" I kick Big Wolf to answer.

"Yes officers, this is the last of the trash we're taking out. We didn't want to interfere with the firefighters."

"You have a card? I have a small job on Long Island that I need done and I like your work ethic. Go ahead, put the trash in the back of the van and give me a card."

I can't believe this shit. This mothafucka wants a card and he's walking with us to the van with Foxy Red inside dressed like a ho and no trash in sight. I grab the cop's arm and lead him away to the front of the van towards the driver's seat.

"I don't think we have any cards left, but give me your cell and I will text you our number."

I pull out my phone and notice my hands are shaking and I'm sweating in the cold. The cop gives me his number, but he doesn't notice my hands. I think I see him gazing into the van and I'm wondering if he sees Red dressed like a ho in what's supposed to be a demo van.

" Goodnight," I'll call I say as I scramble into the front seat.

"9-mm! Drive away now!"

But as he pulls off a stupid black mothafucka steps into the street in front of the van. 9-mm slams on the brakes and Snake's body flies against the back door of the van, knocking it open. Snake's body crashes to the ground as a cop car behind brakes seemingly inches from Snake's body. There's pandemonium in the van.

"Stop and calm down. 9, back up fast."

Wolf reaches his long arm down and hoists and hefts Snake's body back toward the van. We pull and grab and get Snake back inside. Maybe the cops didn't realize it was a body. Thought it was trash. And what's another pile of trash on a Harlem street? 9-mm drives away nice and slow, stopping for a red light at the corner, but we see flashing lights behind us. A siren. Okay, now we'd better jump and run, but the cop car swerves past us, almost side swiping us in their hurry to get somewhere else. They speed off down the street and suddenly I have to laugh. We're all laughing. Switchblade kisses and hugs me as tears roll down her face. Big Wolf pulls out that bottle of cognac and we drink, passing it around as 9-mm drives away.

NINE

Dear God,

Do you know what I miss? I miss Sundays. They were special when I lived with my grandmama. Now every day is the same, but worse than the one before. If I ever have a child, Dear God, I'll make sure to have a special day, so there's something to look forward to. But of course I know I'll never have a child. I know I won't get much beyond childhood myself. I see my future. Bleakness, fear, pain and early death.

It's very cold tonight as I walk into Pam's apartment building on the Upper West Side. My short jacket doesn't protect me from the winds off the Hudson, that dark, evil river. In the lobby there's an old white lady looking at me like I'm going to rob her broke ass. She has this ugly short white hairy dog that's looking at me all fucked up as well. This bitch is staring at me as if I were some kind black ghost. This is one thing I hate about this city, how white people look as if they have never seen a black person before. I hate the way they think a young black person wants to rob their broke ass. I want to say to her, old white bitch I'm a drug dealer ho. I got money. I came to this building to plan a robbery, not to rob you... broke old bitch. I walk to the elevator and this bitch follows behind me walking all slow, with that fucked looking dog.

The elevator door opens and I walk inside. The old ho is walking slower than an old ass turtle with the legs tied., but to my surprise, she gets into the elevator with me. I wish I could just smack the shit out the old bitch with her road map face looking like it was hit by a truck. I should rob that dog from her ass, but that's probably the only friend she has. Or take out Jericho and pistol whip this old bitch right here on the elevator. Staring at me like I'm some kind of monster. The elevator stops on the third floor, the door opens and the old lady says to me with a huge smile, "You have a wonderful night young lady. Excuse me for staring. I was admiring how lovely and beautiful you are." She exits the elevator smiling, her eyes seem to glow.

Those words hit me hard, forcing me to reflect on my life and the cruelty of the ghetto. Suddenly tears well up in my eyes and it takes everything in me to keep from crying. I think to myself what the hell is wrong with me? I don't need to be in a white folks building crying like a bitch. I have to pull myself together quick before this shit stops on the next floor and someone steps into the elevator about to see me cry like a baby. I quickly wipe the tears from my face, wondering what just happened. I know gangstas are not supposed to cry. Obviously we all cry in the dark sometimes, but I'm on an Upper West Side elevator with the lights on exposing my sins and my secretes. I think I will feel a lot better inside the apartment, planning the robbery with Pam and knowing I will be getting some real money to move the hell out of New York. Miles did say all the real gangstas are dead and I'm a real gangsta about to rob some Italians downtown, mothafuckas who created the Mafia. I'm about to put a gun to the head of the Godfather and rob his ass the night of a NYPD party. If that's not some real gangsta shit I don't know what real gangsta shit is.

I knock on Pam's door and she opens it wearing only a white bathrobe with her cop badge pinned to it. She is smiling and fresh as brand new snow. The lights are dim, and Luther Vandross sings "A House Is Not A Home." On the coffee table are a bottle of champagne, two glasses and her gun. She pours us each a glass of champagne. As we drink she kisses me. Opening her bathrobe, she leans back on the couch pulling me to her. As I go to kiss her again she stops me, pushing my head down to her breast. I kiss her dick hard nipples, almost nursing like a baby. She takes her gun from the coffee table, then pushes my face down to her wet pussy. Putting the gun to my head she growls roughly, "Eat my pussy good young bitch." She has me on my knees praying to the love Gods. With the loaded gun at my head, moaning , she says, "Yes, this is how I like raping you underage bitches."

I can't help but think about my Hakeem right about now. And how I would have a much better future with him, on his way to Broadway and Hollywood, than with this crazy bitch with a loaded gun to my head, or Switchblade, who undoubtedly will be a career ghetto hood. Pam moans louder, obviously having an orgasm. She holds my face tight to her pussy, almost smothering me. I feel and taste her milky oily orgasm oozing in my mouth. I'm just at the point of being smothered to death when she lets my head go. I quickly pull away taking a deep breath, gasping for air. Running to the bathroom I gag before I can spit the shit out of my mouth into the toilet. I wash my face and look at myself in the mirror, wondering who I really am. I realize that when I walk through the door there will be no turning back, for better or for worse. But what choices do I have in life? I'm stuck between a sociopath waiting on the couch, and Killa Kim waiting in Harlem. Not to mention Bonnie, whose face I'll never forget. Pam calls me as I look at myself again in the mirror before walking through that door. She's standing in front of the coffee table with two glasses of champagne. She hands me a glass.

"Cheers to the great robbery tomorrow night." We toast, then drink the champagne. She looks at me smiling, totally relaxed, showing no signs of trepidation.

It's twenty-four hours later and I'm still mentally preparing myself for the robbery at the restaurant tonight. I don't have Pam's cool or confidence. The woman has no nerves. And it's so noisy in the apartment I can't think straight. Miles is in the mist of his regular poker party tonight and as usual, most of these niggas is here for the coke, the drinks and the party. I check Jericho again to make sure he's fully loaded. I look at my new ski mask, putting it on again to make sure it fits. My phone rings. Hakeem asks me to stop by for a minute. As hang up the phone Pinch comes to my door high as hell.

"Where you goin this time of night baby girl?"

"I can't sleep with all the noise and all those drunk niggas in the house, so I'm going down to Hakeem's place."

She says okay, but she probably forgets as soon as she walks out the door, high as she is. I'm careful to lock my door behind me on a night like this. The living room seems more like a ghetto nightclub than an apartment. I walk downstairs. Hakeem opens the door before I can remove my hand and motion me inside, holding a finger to his lips. "My mom's asleep."

Then he tries to kiss me. Smiling, probably the only time I've smiled for days, I push him away. Instead of a kiss I give him a wad of cash.

"Take this cash and hold on to it for me until I get back. If I don't come back for it, keep it, and split it with the crew."

I pull out a photo of Pam and hand it to him.

"Her name, address and phone number are on the back of the photo. If I don't come back that bitch is the one who's responsible." Most of these hood rats around here are not going anywhere, but you have a future and are going places, so if I don't ever see you again my advice is to stay away from the bullshit and the haters as much as you can and really focus on your acting. Let that be your vehicle to get the fuck out of here."

And luckily for Hakeem, before my lecture can go any further, I get a text from Pam. "Giorgio's is closing. Get into a cab now." I hug Hakeem goodbye and walk out the door.

I leave the cab a few blocks from the restaurant so I can walk off my nerves a little. Butterflies dance in my stomach. I guess I finally made it to the super bowl. As I get closer I can hear the roar of the crowd. I hear them, calling my name. TKO… TKO.. TKO. Walking past Giorgio's I peer into the window. Nothing. It's empty. And then my phone bleeps again. Another text from Pam. "It's time. Move and come through the back door now." This is a really smart bitch because she is not texting me from her phone, but from some throw away phone she gets in New Jersey. Another bleep. Another text. "Back door. Now!" So I run down the ally putting on my mask. I open the back door of the empty kitchen. I'm almost hyperventilating pulling out Jericho as I run towards the office in the back. There is Pam with Marcello, counting the money. I raise my gun and yell "Put your hands up. Freeze."

I throw Marcello a bag. "Put the money in the bag now!" Without a word he stuffs money in the bag dropping shit on the floor.

Pam, with her hands up says, "I'm a cop and you don't want to do this!"

"Thanks for telling me that because I'm shooting your ass if you put your hands down!"

Suddenly I hear laughter in the kitchen. I spin around to see the rest of the family in the office. And they see me. Panicking, I look at Pam and cry, "Oh shit, Pam, what should I do?"

Pam yells, "You bitch!" at me and pulls out her gun. I duck out of the way thinking she is about to shoot me. But she shoots Marcello in the head at point blank range. The rest of the family are shocked. She immediately turns on the father, shooting him in the back as he tries to escape. The mother and daughter scream and try to back out of the office into the kitchen. Pam yells for me to shoot, but I can't move. Pam runs past, knocking me aside. I turn and follow her into the kitchen and the mother and daughter trip over each other falling to the kitchen floor. They turn crawling backwards , scrambling on their hands and knees. I can't breathe. All of the air is sucked out of me. This was not the plan, murder in the first degree. The mother and daughter are sprawled on the floor holding hands, begging Pam for their lives. I look down again and I see my great grandma and Jamaican Bonnie crawling across the floor with them, begging for mercy also. Jericho screams, "Shoot this bitch. If you don't you're next!" Bang… bang… bang… In cold blood Pam executes the two women. The she turns her rage on me, slapping me in the face, bringing me back to cold reality. Murder, she wrote.

We hear Police sirens heading in the direction of the restaurant. Pam walks over to the mother and daughter and puts two more bullets in their heads. We turn and run back into the office. Marcello is lying on the bag of money so we roll him over and I grab the bag. All the money is soaked in Marcello's blood.

Pam says, "Leave it. Let's go."

As we run out the back door another cop walks in, gun drawn. He does not see me in the corner behind Pam. He seems to know Pam and starts to say something when she shoots him in face. We walk over his body, out the door, as Pam puts on a ski mask. We run down the dark ally, and over a gate between two apartment buildings. We run between buildings to another gate. And finally we stop and remove our ski masks. We jump over the gate onto an empty street. Then Pam's real phone rings.

"No, I'll be there in a minute," she says, her voice distressed.

Pam turns to me. "That was my partner all freaked out. He said I have to get down to the restaurant. Go straight home TKO and don't lose your composure. I've got this."

She turns around heading back to the restaurant. I wait until she walks away disappearing down the street before I head back to the scene of the crime, taking a page from her book.

I walk across the street from the restaurant and see spectators and cops everywhere. Pam is inside, hugging and consoling the only remaining son, who wasn't there, so she couldn't kill him. Wow that crazy bitch is colder than ice. She executed damn near the whole family one minute ago, now she's consoling the grieving survivor the next. That's some really cold shit and I guess dead men and women don't tell no tales. What a horrible waste. After all that we still could not take the money.

Some cops walk through the crowd and I tense up knowing they are looking for me and Pam. I hear on the radio of a cop walking by that they are looking for two black males wearing black jackets and black pullover hats. I'm thinking half the black mothafuckas in New York meet that description. I immediately take off my black pullover cap, revealing my braids. I pull out the red lipstick that some bitch was giving out as a sample on the street today and smear my lips. There is a fat black bitch standing next to me wearing big fake gold earrings. I feel like snatching them off her ears and putting them on mine.

The reason I agreed to help this bitch rob the restaurant was for the money so I could move down South and find another life. It looks like the only place I will be moving to anytime soon is the nearest electric chair and not the kind in Big Wolf's apartment. Damn, if the police ever find out it was one of their own who did this they'll sentence this bitch to execution six of the seven days of the week. Something tells me I better start writing my autobiography now, cause I might not have much longer. If Pam goes down I know she'll take me with her. And even if the cops don't find us, these are Italians this crazy bitch just put on ice. They could be mob connected and if they get Pam, she'll give them me for sure If they create a museum for gangtas, Pam's photograph could be right next to Al Capone's.

A bleep. Another text. Hakeem. "My mom just left for work. Want to come over?" I text back "hell yes." I need someone to talk to tonight. There's a mob scene of blue and I don't see Pam. I wonder how she is talking her way out of this. People know that she moonlighted at Giorgio's. I walk down the street calm on the outside, but very much afraid on the inside, wondering how long will it be before the cops break down my door. And what frightens me just as much, more, is Pam. She's a psycho and I am the only witness to her crime. Why didn't she shoot me? She could have. I was a trembling wreck. I couldn't have run because I couldn't move. What will she want from me? What else will she want me to do? Trembling, I flag down an African gypsy cab. The driver asks me immediately what happened and why all the cops' cars. I tell him I think a restaurant was robbed and people where shot. Then he says to me. "That's why I don't pick up just anyone in my car."

"I hear that my brother, it's better to be safe than sorry," I say...

What's truly terrifying is that Pam didn't show any emotion at all. She didn't even get that angry about me screwing up and calling out her name. My stupidity got those people killed, but it happened so fast there was nothing I could do. I said the name Pam and the next thing I heard was bang. The elevator in my building smells like pee, welcome back to the hood. On Hakeem's floor there's a little puddle outside the elevator door. Animal? Human? He comes to the door looking like a little boy with his pajamas on. He has the TV on in the living room. There is a female reporter in front of the restaurant talking about the shooting and interviewing Pam, of all people. The reporter hands Pam the mike and she says to the camera.

"We will find the animals who did this to my dear friends. And we will show them the same mercy he showed to Giogio's family."

I ask Hakeem to please cut off the TV before he realizes that's Pam, whose photograph I gave him.

"Are you okay TKO? You look a little weird and it's not just the lipstick."

"I'm okay, " I lie, telling him to put on some music.

He puts on Adele's "I Set Fire To The Rain." That's no bullshit because I saw a bitch tonight, who set fire to the rain. Yeah, she set some asses on fire tonight. Hakeem takes my coat off and drops it on the floor. He starts kissing me, but I push him away. He grabs me, tackling me to the couch, then puts his tongue in my mouth. He begins tearing my clothes off, kissing very intensely. I can feel myself getting excited, pulling him towards me. He pulls off my pants and panties and sticks his fingers inside me. Young as he is, he knows what to do. After the kind of night I've had, I need a brother like him to wash my sins away. He penetrates me setting fire to the rain. I begin to cry and kiss him at the same time as Adele sings.

'Cause there's a side to you that I never knew,
    I never knew
But I set fire to the rain
Watch it pour as I touched your face
Let it burn while I cried
Cause I heard it screaming out your name
    out your name

I set fire to the rain
And I threw us into the flames
Where I felt somethin' die 'cause I knew that
That was the last time the last time

Amazingly I slept, or thought I did, but now I'm awake, sweating and although I know it's not possible, that it's only Pinch and me and Miles, I hear moaning, "Please, please, please." And then I remember my dream, or am I still dreaming? I was locked in a dark room and rats were everywhere. The door opened and I was glad, because I thought someone had come to save me, or kill the rats, or something. But instead a very tall, very thin, hooded figure entered, man, woman, I couldn't tell. But it knew my name And called it, "Jean," and reached out with a long, thin, prong and everywhere it touched me my skin opened and freezing, putrid green scum oozed out.

Stumbling, I walk into the living room, which resembles my dream. Plastic cups, liquor bottles, coke bags litter the couch, the floor, the tables, the backs of chairs. Chicken bones lie in nasty heaps wherever folks reached down and dropped them. There are scorch marks in the plastic covers that Pinch uses to save her upholstery. A rotten pussy smell hangs over the room, like burning incense in a crack house. Pinch has a lot of work to do when she wakes up sometime this afternoon. That's what happens when she gets high, things get out of hand. Miles won't do anything today but count money and yell at her to clean the place up.

But I have to hurry. It's a workday and Miles will be pissed if I'm still around when he finally gets his old ass out of bed. Outside, my heart pounds. I know the cops could bum-rush me at any moment and my life could be over. Dying in prison would be worse for me than dying young, so if they come Jericho will take me home. A shoot out would be a blessing. I can't help stopping at the newsstand. Pam's superbowl game is all over the front pages of every paper in town. We even made The Metro Section of The New York Times. I buy all the newspapers. They all say the same thing. The Police Commissioner assures the citizens of New York that the perpetrators of this heinous crime will be captured. So they can give them their 22 inch, 7 pound, Vince Lombardi Trophy? I guess when they send the handcrafted Tiffany trophy off to be engraved, Me and Pam's name will be at the very top, along with the date, time and address of the scene of the crime.

Kurt Anthony

Today I'm seeing Miss Mamai, who was a good friend of my great grandma. I have known her all of my life and remember when she used to wear these big beautiful hats to church. She and my great grandma sat side by side on the pew and no one else but me could fit there because their hats were so big. And they were big ladies too. After church other ladies would join us at Sylvia's Restaurant. I remember I couldn't wait for dessert sometimes and great grandma would order dessert first for me. My stomach would be so full that I couldn't eat my meal afterwards, but that was okay with great grandma, because she took it home and gave it to me for dinner that night. I love Miss Mamai because she reminds me of so many fond memories of my childhood. She is so much like great grandmama, sweet, loving , kind with never a bad thing to say about anything or anybody. It makes me sad sometimes when I come here. It reminds me of the life I used to have, a beautiful, quiet, stable, home, eating dinner at the same time every night, praying before I went to bed and listening to grandmama reading me bedtime stories before putting me to sleep. I long for those days and all the delicious smells floating through the house when she made those fabulous meals. But what's the point of looking back? I don't want to look back to other times, when grandmama died and I had to move in with my mother. I don't let myself remember that.

Miss Mamai opens the door with her customary smile.

"It's smells good in here Miss Mamai, what'cha cooking?"

"You just in time honey, I have a fresh peach cobbler that just came out of the oven. Follow me into the kitchen, let's eat pie."

"Yes Ma'am."

On the kitchen table the three New York papers are open to the execution story. I don't know what to do, think, or feel right now. I feel numb, like a truck drove a big hole right through me. Lord, what I'm gonna do now? Gang banging up in Harlem is one thing , killing an Italian family downtown is some whole other deep shit. They give mothafuckas the electric chair for shit like that. Killing mothafuckas like that is not my style. That's why I took out Snake on the down low, to eliminate the drama. There's drama now. The Mayor is already calling for the guillotine.

"Darlin do you want milk or tea with your peach cobbler honey?"

I want to say I need a pound of crack with that please, but I know she doesn't smoke. So I just say milk. She serves us the cobbler and milk and I take a bite out of the pie.

"Oh Miss Mamai this is so good. It's delicious. Thank you. I'm so glad I came at this time."

"You know it's always my pleasure honey. You have grown into a fine, beautiful young lady and I know your great grandmother would be so proud of you."

"Thank you for saying that Miss Mamai. I hope you know how much I enjoy coming here to see you."

"And I enjoy seeing you as well Jean. You know, you have not changed much since you were a little girl. You still have the sweet little babyface and those big shiny eyes."

"Thank you, Miss Mamai.'

I'm glad to know there are still some beautiful black people like Miss Mamai left in the world. But I fear what's going to happen to us as a people once Miss Mamai and Professor Weeks' generations die. What will become of the younger generation, me, my generation, that lacks the same pedigree? Me. What kind of example am I? How do I honor my grandmama?

"Honey I know you read here in the papers this morning about that robbery and mass murder at Giorgio's Restaurant last night."

"Yes Ma'am, I did."

"Lord have mercy, I wonder sometimes what has gotten into this world with all this senseless violence. Help me Jesus! They said they are looking for two young black males who a witness saw running away from the scene of the crime. They are asking anyone with any information to come forward. My

Lord, those poor people, everyone in the family was murdered except for a son... my Lord!

But you know the difference between my generation and your generation honey?"

"No, Ma'am," I say wondering.

"The difference is that my generation was afraid to die, your generation is not afraid to kill. And sometimes that's a good thing, it all depends."

I'm stunned wondering what has gotten into Miss Mamai.

"You see honey, I was born way before your time in Money, Mississippi. We black people down South caught nothing but hell. The only job a black woman could get was working in some racist cracker's house where you were paid nothing, treated like dirt and forced to use the bathroom in a nasty, sticking, wooden box in the backyard in the rain, sleet or snow. And after you had raised their children from birth and those babies turned nineteen or twenty, they became the boss and started calling you a nigger and all. So I've learnt over the years it's better to be feared and respected than to get your butt kicked every day."

I'm thinking Miss Mamai has been drinking or smoking or something before I came over, because this doesn't sound like her.

"Child let me tell you this story. I was a teenager in 1955 in Money Mississippi when a fourteen year old named

Emmett Till came there from Chicago to visit his cousin, who lived right next door to me and my family. When I met him he was laughing and showing off. That same day Emmett and his young cousin went to Bryant grocery store to buy candy. When they were leaving, Emmett started showing off and then whistled at Carolyn Bryant, who was working behind the counter. When they got outside, Emmett pulled out his wallet, flashing a picture of a white girl, claiming that she was his girl friend. In the early morning of the next day Roy Bryant and his half brother J. W. Milam pulled up to Reverend Moses Wright's house, where Emmett was staying. The two white men banged in the door, found Emmett in the bedroom and asked Emmett "Are you the nigger we looking for who whistled at Miss Carolyn Bryant?"

"Yeah."

"They dragged him out to the truck to be identified by Carolyn Bryant. Then they threw Emmett into the truck and warned Reverend Moses in front of his family, "If you tell anybody about this you won't live to be 65." Emmett Till was never seen alive after that. When they found his decomposed body there were massive injuries to the face and head, including a missing eye and ear, a gunshot wound in the temple, and a hole in the skull so large that part of the skull was missing. The body was found in a river, weighed down by a cotton gin fan tied with barbed wire around his neck.

When they shipped his body to Chicago his mother insisted that the coffin be opened. So for four days about 100,000 people came through the funeral home to see Emmett's body. They said the sight and condition of the body caused grown men to cry and women to faint. His murderers went to trial but were acquitted. Then they sold their confessions to Look Magazine. That outraged people. That was one of the incidents that started the civil rights movement."

Wow, I look down at what is left of the peach cobbler, speechless. I don't know what to say after that.

"You know honey, I don't believe this story that they are telling us in the paper about this was a robbery gone bad by two black boys. They said the money was left in a bloody bag and they didn't take it. I believe this was a cold blooded hit by the mob. The papers said they all were shot in the head twice. These black kids don't know how to shoot that well. They're out there missing their targets and killing the wrong people every day. And besides, strange as it seems, I knew the family that owned the restaurant and the Lieutenant in charge of the precinct who was having the party there for his son-in-law last night. Before I retired, I was a housekeeper for an Italian family on Long Island, not too far from where Giorgio and his family lived. And it was no secret then that they had strong ties to the mob. And Lieutenant Coppo, who had the party, I've known him for years. He had two partners, one is named Louis Giovanni. Giovanni's retired, but was arrested recently in Las Vegas on charges of murder, obstruction of justice, drug distribution and money laundering. They also identified him as a hit man for mob. He did thirteen murders the police say, including killing mobsters. Didn't you see this on the news, honey?

"The other partner was Don Giordino, who's in prison for helping the mob run a 30 million dollar internet gambling operation out of a Queens strip club. Since I retired I've become quite a news junkie, CNN, MSNBC, Fox News, Nancy Grace. You mean to tell me the Lieutenant didn't know what kind of company he was keeping? It was also no secret that Giorgio had a huge gambling problem and owed money to the wrong people. That was no botched robbery. Lord, it was a Mafia hit and I guarantee you the cops were involved"

I don't know whether to laugh, cry, shoot myself or just go jump off the bridge. I came here to collect the numbers from Miss Mamai, a church going, God fearing woman. And she's serving me peach cobbler and giving me lesson on who's who in New York's crime underworld. My God, not only is that crazy Pam a freak, but she could also be a Mafia hit woman. I did say that her photograph should be right next to Al Capone's. Now I'm thinking after I leave here maybe I should head straight to the airport.

"Honey are you all right? Would you like some more peach cobbler?"

Hell no, I'm thinking. I need to find out where the nearest crack house is. Hopefully one is next door, cause I need to buy every rock in the house.

"What do you think? Do you think I will get lucky today and hit the numbers?"

I'm thinking with my luck it'll be a miracle if I make it to tomorrow.

"Here you go honey, here is my numbers. Blow on it for good luck would you ?"

I walk out the door praying I don't hear anymore stories today. Maybe I should go down and join the Peace Corps in the morning and if get lucky they'll ship me off to Siberia. Or even better, join the army and immediately get deployed to the war zone in Afghanistan. Maybe I'll get lucky, fall off the truck and get captured by the Taliban. As I try humoring myself, my phone rings and I see it's the devil herself calling me.

"We need to get together tonight," Pam says. "Cover our tracks."

She sounds almost giddy, not scared at all. This bitch isn't human. This is the first time in my life I need to talk to somebody about what is happening to me , but who? This kind of information is dynamite in the wrong hands and TNT in the others. If I tell that crazy ass Miles, no telling what he might do. A nigga like that could kill ya or march you down to the police station, either way it won't be good. Okay, say the police believe me that the devil make me do it? Where could I run and hide from the mob? The only place I know is hell and I'm here already. I have no place to run, no place to hide, Kim on one side, Pam on the other.

Funny how my tired old building looks different to me now. The niggas I used to hate looking at, I'm glad to see. That piss in the elevator is not so bad after all. It sure beats the smell of blood. And these loud, bad ass kids running around the projects who mamas don't want them, maybe they just have a lot of energy. Inside my apartment, James Brown's "Get On Up" greets me at the door. Miles is at the table with Cat Fish, Mo Green and this old gee named Baldey, who I haven't seen in a while. I walk to the table and hand Miles the money and numbers. Cat Fish looks at me and laughs.

"Hey Ug-Mo, you ain't going to say hello? Is that you and your gang I've been reading about in the newspaper today? It was your gang, right, who went downtown and killed all those peckerwoods, right? The papers said one of the gang bangers they saw running away was short, slim with long braids under a black skull cap. That sounds exactly like you. You are short, slim with long braids that you normally wear under a black skull cap every day, except for today. Why is that? Where is your black skull cap today? When I read the newspaper you was the first person who came to mind. And I watched you leave the house last night one hour before those peckerwoods got shot."

He's laughing, pointing his finger at me. I'm thinking this is some scary shit, did someone really see me running away or is this some shit that Pam is putting out to set me up? Either way it's not good, because it was me running away, whether or not this old crazy nigga is fucking with me or not. "Hello Houston I think I have a problem." I force a laugh as I walk away.

"You got me Catfish. I'm big time now."

I know this old nigga is just playing. He thinks Street Queens is just a bunch of girls playing dress up. My phone rings and I see it's Switchblade.

"Can you come over baby?"

"Later Switch. I've go to make a run for Miles now."

Another call. This time it's Foxy Red.

"Oh, My, God," she shrieks into my ear. "Was it you? Downtown? Oh, My, God. I know a real killer! The description of the person running from Giorgio's was you TKO. Oh, My, God!"

"If it was me Foxy, you and the other ladies would have been right by my side," I laugh.

"If only," she says. "That would have really been fun."

This girl is obviously much more twisted than I thought. My bad. I assume that folks with money don't need anything else. Miss Foxy Red obviously does.

"When are we going to kill someone else?"

"I thought Jewish girls can't do stuff like that," I joke.

"That was before we killed somebody."

"You didn't kill anybody. You just ran around naked, screaming at the top of your lungs."

"Talk to you later," she laughs and clicks off.

A few hours later I'm heading over to Pam's. I wonder what kind of bullshit this is going to be. The best way in my opinion to cover your tracks is not to get your sins plastered across the papers in the first place. When I got rid of Snake, I didn't try to kill him in broad daylight like they tried to kill me. I waited and took that nigga out when the time was right and buried his ass so deep underground the worms won't be able to find that nigga.

At Pam's apartment building I meet that same old white lady walking her dog.

"Nice to see you again," she says.

I can see she wants to chat, but I don't have the patience for anything but confronting Pam.

"Be careful dear. That shooting the other night really unsettled me. It's like the 1970s all over again. Pretty young girls like you have to be especially careful."

"Thank you Ma'am. I'll stay alert."

This time when Pam opens the door she's wearing her cop uniform.

"Just in time for dinner, I just ordered some Chinese food."

I look around and listen for any sounds out of the ordinary. I have two guns stashed on me ready for anything that might jump off. And I'm not having sex with this crazy bitch tonight or any other night after this. Hell no, the days of this bitch fucking me with a gun to my head are over. I don't care if we died and went to heaven together, I'm still not fucking with this bitch. I don't know why I was fucking with police in the first place. This crazy bitch is not only a cop, she's likely a hit woman for the Mafia. That's why she shot the whole family. She's not crazy like I thought. She was doing a job. If her boss at the precinct is down with the mob, the apple don't fall far from the tree. This is the kind of bitch that would have me eating her pussy then pull the trigger as she's coming. My great grandma used to say "A rich man's death is an object lesson in the poverty of a life lived without spiritual meaning." It took me years to understand what that meant. But you don't have to be rich to be a spiritually depraved mothafucka. Most niggas I know fall into that category, especially the ones in blue uniforms.

"What are you drinking, wine, water or soda?"

"I'll take a soda."

I follow Pam to the kitchen to make sure she doesn't poison my drink. As she pours the soda she looks directly into my eyes.

"What were you thinking last night when you blew my cover asking me what you should do? You supposed to be a gangsta, remember? What do you think happens when you get caught with your hands in the cookie jar?"

"You said the coast would be clear and the only person that would be there would be drunk Marcello putting away the money. You didn't say anything about what to do if someone walked in during the robbery."

I know I sound like a little girl.

"But I did tell you to start shooting after I took Marcello out, before they could make it the door?"

I don't say anything. I still can't believe she turned the restaurant into a killing field and thinks that's okay. This is not Prohibition and we are not Dutch Schultz and Al Capone.

"Answer me. Didn't I tell you to start shooting after you fucked up everything? I don't appreciate having to clean up your mess!"

"For God sake's, Pam, I'm only sixteen years old. I didn't go there to kill anyone. The reason I agreed to do what we did in the first place was to get some money to create a better life for myself. Not to get in deeper into something I won't be able to get out of."

Angry, she jumps all over me, spitting in my face as she talks.

"Listen young dumb bitch! You are not the only one with plans here and not the only one with something to lose. I know white people in high places and they are grooming me to become the first black female Police Commissioner."

"Police Commissioner?" I laugh.

"That's some crazy fantasy Pam. Mafia soldier, maybe."

"For a supposedly smart girl you're really naïve, Jean. There's a whole world of corruption that you obviously can't imagine, stuck as you are in your limited ghetto world. I am a smart, young, good looking member of New York's finest. And I'm female and I'm black. Who better to symbolize New York's diversity and commitment to all its citizens? What better way to silence the protests about police on black crime? And if I happen to manage some inside work for my supporters along the way, they will be that much more persuasive when my time comes. It's not my time yet, obviously. But in a few years, after several promotions, when the new Mayor wants to promote from within the

Department, I'll be at the head of the line, put there by my champions, who are also the Mayor's big, secret donors. There's scenes and behind the scenes, little Jean. And everything important happens off stage. And I will not let all of that go up in smoke because you open your big, scared mouth and fuck everything up. I had no choice but to clean up your mess. So now you don't have any choice but to help me make this right!"

I'm stunned by what Pam has told me and more frightened than ever. She's right. I'm a child, a babe in this land of evil and corruption where Pam struts her stuff.

"What do I have to do now?" I whisper.

"Simple. Just finish what you started. I need you to go out of town until the smoke clears. But first you are going to help us rob a very successful hair salon with a high profile clientele."

"You must be kidding, right? This is a joke, right?"

"Wake up bitch! Do I look like I'm a comedian?"

I'm speechless. They haven't even put the Italian bodies on ice yet. And the ink hasn't dried on the headlines and she wants to rob, or should I say try and rob another place. I would not rob another place with that bitch even if it were a kindergarten and the kids handed us their candy money as soon as we walked in the door. I don't get it after what Pam just told me. Why do this stupid stuff? Why doesn't she just work her job? But she's going on.

"I get my hair done at this salon and the owner doesn't like paying taxes. So she offers a 10% discount for clients paying cash and she keeps a lot of cash on hand to make change, pay her distributors, who also don't mind keeping some things secret from Uncle Sam. Once a month a group of NBA housewives come in a group to get their hair done. They wear a lot of very expensive jewelry. That's the day I need you to rob the salon. I'll be getting my hair done on that day also, so when you come I'll be sitting in the chair waiting to get robbed along with everyone else."

Now I'm starting to wonder if Pam is crazy or if she's just stupid, because if she's crazy that would explain it.

"I have two friends coming over for dinner tonight, Trouble and his cousin, Cognac. They are the ones you will be doing the Salon job with."

"How do you know these guys? Are you sure you can trust them?"

"Don't worry about where I know them from. If I couldn't trust them they wouldn't be coming. You just listen up when they get here. I've planned this to the last detail. Don't fuck this one up this time. When you and my two boys run in pulling out guns all those bitches are going to start shitting in their panties. You just make sure the only thing you leave those NBA bitches is their underwear."

The door bell rings.

"Guys, this is TKO, TKO this is Trouble and his cousin Cognac." We shake hands and the only thing I can think about is heading straight down to the Greyhound bus station once I leave here. I started off initiating mothafuckas into my own gang, next thing I knew I woke up one morning in her gang. How the fuck did that happen? I thought this bitch was already in a gang, the New York City Police Department.

We sit at the dinner table passing around Chinese food. Cognac pulls out two 24 ounce Coors from a plastic bag and hands one to Trouble. Trouble looks at me like a pervert and asks, "Do you have a sister?"

"I do… what age are you thinking about, anything over ten years old?" I answer sarcastically.

As we pass the food around, I look at Pam, trying to read her mind, trying to see any signs of fear, panic or remorse. The only thing I see is a look and a stare that can set fire to ice. She's a lioness who would eat her own newborn baby. The old Chicago mob would have loved this black bitch. They would have viewed her as an equal opportunity killa, black, white, male, female, makes no difference to her. Pam takes a deep breath and knocks on her glass with a knife, like she doesn't already have everyone's attention.

"This is the situation at Cleopatra Hair Salon. Nicky, the owner, has some of her high profile clients coming this Saturday. There are going to be a couple of rappers and at least four to six NBA wives, executives, two Broadway producers and the like. You get the picture. The rappers may come in with security and the NBA wives might come together with one bodyguard. That's okay, because Nicky does not allow guns in her salon of course, except for mine, because I'm a police officer and an old friend. If I weren't I couldn't afford to have my hair done at her place. So I do her favors and act as security on her big days when the shoes those bitches wear cost more than my monthly salary. Now Nicky don't like paying taxes. So she's going to have cash there from a few days before as well, because she also doesn't like going to the bank every day. When she does deposit the money, it's in various accounts. She has accounts in her mother's name, her father's name, her sister's name, her brother's name, her dog's name, you name it, she has one. Uncle Sam is not getting shit if she can help it. She comes from a family of old school hustlers from Harlem. The cash is kept in a safe inside her office. This the plan. I send Trouble a text on one of these new phones I have here. You come waving guns like crazy killer mothafuckas. You tell everyone, 'Don't move, shut up and no one will get hurt.' Immediately handcuff any security and take the customers' wallets. Now they know that you know where they live."

Pam hands Trouble a photograph and says, "This is the owner Nicky in her blonde weave. I want you to grab the bitch. TKO and Cognac, I want you two to take the customers, staff and security to the back of the salon, lay them on the floor face down. TKO, I want you to grab a bitch, turn her over and take your gun butt and knock that bitch's front teeth out. That way everyone knows you mean business and no one will try anything stupid. Then I want you, Cognac, to go to the front watching the door as Trouble takes Nicky to her office to open the safe. TKO, I want you to make sure that you take everybody's shit, all the jewelry and the pocketbooks, then dump the contents inside a bag. Make sure you get all the rings off the fingers. And make sure plastic cuffs are on all the guys, faggots included. I want you all in and out in less than ten minutes. A yellow cab will be waiting for you when you walk outside. And Trouble I want you to cuff and duct tape that Nicky after she opens the safe. And don't forget your ski masks. Oh yeah, one more thing. Don't forget to take the diamond ring off Nicky's finger."

I look over at Trouble and Cognac with the scars on their faces, the no redemption in their eyes and the twelve deadly sins on their breath. They look like hardcore ex-cons who've been fucking niggas in prison who look Mike Tyson all their lives.

"TKO, do you have any questions?" Pam asks me.

"Ahhhh…. yeah. Is there a back exit, just in case something happens out front? Because me being in the back puts me at a disadvantage if something jumps off out front or the cops come or whatever."

"First of all, the only cop that is gonna be there is me. And second, I'm going to be a customer there lying in the cut to make sure everything jumps off right and no one does anything stupid. I need everyone exiting at the same time and jumping in the cab with the money. Simple as that… So forget about a back exit escape. There is none. Does everybody understand that?"

The Greyhound bus station is looking better and better to me right now. Hopefully the bus I jump on can grow wings and get me out of town fast. I wish I had the money for a plane ticket to anywhere.

"We are going to do some practice runs first. I want to make sure everyone knows exactly what to do and when and how to do it. I'm going to give you a blueprint of the salon layout and we are going to do some walkthroughs. I'm going to coach you on how to do this right."

Later, I find myself at the Port Authority Bus Terminal. I don't know why I came here, I'm not going anywhere. Maybe I just came down here to look at the buses, imagine what it would be like traveling on the road. For a few minutes I convince myself that I can do it. Just leave. I have a little money. I can afford a ticket to somewhere. But after I get who knows where, then what? I'd be another young girl on the street. At least here I know who my enemies are and my friends. Do I have any friends?

TEN

Dear God,

So this is the way the world works. The media isn't talking about poor Bonnie anymore. There's much more dramatic crime to report. Her parents and I are probably the only ones who even remember her now. My misfortune, or my saving grace, is that I remember everything and everyone who died before my eyes. I remember their eyes, their terror, their pain, their confusion. I remember their smells, because fear has a smell and once you experience it you can't get it out of your nose. I am lost Dear God. I am truly lost. All I can beg for if you're truly wasting time with this sinner, is mercy.

It's Thursday morning and I'm still with the boys in the hood. Still running numbers, getting older, looking over my shoulders as shit gets colder. The crazy bitch grows bolder and this drama that I'm in is not over. I got 48 hours before that clock starts ticking, stopping that moment in time when blood might flow again. This is not the life I chose, but what was given to me. And given the chance I will survive, the survival of the fittest. These ghettos are like Russian gulags with no place to hide. They're surrounded by that invisible wall longer than the Great Wall of China. More impenetrable than the Iron Curtain. I'm riffing, amusing myself as I move through the hood. Who am I bullshitting, myself? Of course I chose this life. Some people I know who live here are still happy in school, playing basketball, producing talent shows, studying. I'm Queen of The Street Queens because I want to be. I'm just in over my head now. I didn't anticipate that is all.

"Hey black bitch! We know you walk around with money from the numbers in your pocket. We gonna run up on you and rob yo ass one day real soon."

A young nigga passing by in a car yells out to me as I walk up 7th Ave. I hate collecting from Shelly. She lives in one of the most violent project buildings in New York City, maybe the country. Young niggas kill each other off there like they're getting paid for it. I don't know why they just don't dress in Klan robes and start burning crosses. Quiet as it's kept those are the young bucks who're really killing more niggas than the Klan.

The elevator in Shelly's building is called the turtle for obvious reasons. Actually it's slower than a turtle if you ask me. When the door finally opens sad looking folks step out. I'm talking Negroes with the blues. I get on the elevator with more blues singers, the lights blink on and off as the elevator goes up. Suddenly the elevator jerks like it's about blow up. The lights go completely out and I feel some mothafucka's hand feeling my ass up. But I'm afraid to move my hands off the money and push the hand away. The elevator stops, leaving us in the dark. What the fuck? Some nigga is having a field day feeling up my ass. I pray these lights come back so I can see who it is and smack 'em. Bam the light comes back I immediately look back and this little bad ass kid got his hand on my ass laughing. His mother slaps his hand away as the turtle starts to move again. We could have been half way to heaven by now as slow as this elevator is. I finally make it to Shelly's floor and that bad ass kid and his mom follow me off the elevator. I walk down the hall and knock on Shelly's door as that little kid walks past me. Shelly comes to the door looking like she just got out of the bed.

"What time is it?" she asks, closing the door behind me. I see smoke coming from the kitchen like it's on fire.

"It's noon. What the fuck is going on in the kitchen?"

"I left a pot on the stove all night and I need new batteries for the smoke alarm."

"No shit," I say looking around her funky ass apartment.

"Do you have the numbers and the money ready? I need to get the fuck out of here."

Shelly hands me what I need.

"You have a blessed day, okay?" I run out the door coughing. I stash everything away walking to the turtle. I push the button and wait and wait and wait. After what seems like hours, the turtle arrives carrying what looks like an army of refugees on board. The turtle stops on the next floor picking up more people from the camp. The door closes, but I can hear a loud argument below us. When the elevator door opens Kim and her Diva gang enter, arguing so heatedly they don't see me in the crowd. I push people aside and quickly move to the back left corner of the elevator. My heart starts to beat so fiercely against my chest I'm surprised folks don't notice. Kim is animated, screaming at her crew, four bitches and that black nigga who ran me down in the streets.

"Listen now. None of you have done anything for me lately. Snake is missing in action and y'all niggas ain't found out shit yet."

The door closes and I pull my hood up over my face and look down, praying they don't notice me. Sweat streams down my arm pits.

"And that bitch Ginger, she knows where the fuck my brother is at. The last place he was seen was at her club with one of her girls. And you mean to tell me the only thing the bitch has to say is that she don't know where he is? Y'all stupid mothafuckas believe that she owes my brother money and don't want to pay, so she sets my brother up. Fuck what you heard!"

The turtle stops a few floors down and more people enter, crowding us tightly into our spots. Kim and her crew move back and oh my God she moves and stops right next to me. I slightly turn my head so my face almost touches the elevator wall. I put my finger on the triggers of both of my guns, Jericho and my new snub nose 32. This bitch is screaming all over me, pushing me against the wall.

"Since y'all mothafuckas didn't do the job right, I hired an outside contractor. His crew is over at Ginger's apartment right now yo, pulling that bitch's teeth out with pliers one by one until she tells them where Snake is."

Shit. If I can make it off the turtle alive I've got to get to Ginger quick before they kill her or she bleeds to death. The legacy of the ghetto will not be its capacity to contain huge populations and to incapacitate one generation after the next. The legacy of the ghetto is how successful it is at turning hearts to stone. But my heart was forged from Siberian steel, and strengthened by hell's kitchen furnace flames for sixteen cold years. So if Kim notices me, I'm shooting the bitch point blank in the face with both barrels. That'll give the Mortician some work to do before the funeral. My fingers are on the triggers. My mind is with Ginger. My heart is pounding so fast I feel dizzy. I feel I'm about to have a stroke. The sweat pouring from my face is running into my eyes, setting them on fire. The lights start to flicker again and the elevator stops between floors again. Kim is so close to me I can feel her soft breast against my arm. The light continues to flicker on and off. Kim calms down some and she says to her crew:

"You see this weird mothafucka right next to me"

And I hear Jericho yelling, "Let me come all over this bitch now!"

The elevator starts moving down again as I hear Kim say, "You are one weird mothafucka."

I say to Jericho, "You right my brother. It is time for you to come." I take a deep breath, getting ready to shoot Kim in the face. I wait for my cue. I wait for the bitch to open her mouth again.

"Hey Nigga I'm talk…," she says. I don't even glance up to see if she's talking to me. I inhale and turn as I pull out my guns and everything else moves in slow motion. It's time to see whose side God is on today. As I pull out Jericho and my 32 snub to release some hell and fury when the elevator door opens into the lobby. Somebody screams, "He's got a gun, run!"

Everyone panics, running out of the elevator in all directions. Kim and her crew disappear in the crowd so fast I almost shoot the wrong bitch. I put my guns away, running out of the building to the streets and running to Ginger's apartment. I find a cab and call Big Wolf.

"Call 9-mm and both of you meet me at Ginger's apartment as fast as you can. And bring your guns."

I call Ginger but the call goes directly to voicemail, as I worried it would. Big Wolf comes along just as I exit the cab and I bring him up to speed. Because Ginger's is the only apartment in her building there's no one to buzz us in, so Big Wolf slams against the door and, like in a movie, it cracks. Before he's even inside Big Wolf shouts, "Police, open the door now or we are coming in shooting!"

I think I hear screams as we race up the stairs and push into Ginger's loft. Ginger, naked, is tied to a chair, her arms stretched behind her, her legs twisted around the legs of the chair. She's bleeding from every orifice in her face, but she's alive. I check her mouth. She has her teeth.

"Don't worry about my teeth honey. They're false. I lost my own the first year I wrestled."

"Ginger!" I am so happy she's okay I hug her before I untie her. "Let me help you put something on. Then we'll call an ambulance."

Her attackers are long gone, of course, out the back fire escape the minute they heard us at the door.

"You guys take her to hospital. I have to finish collecting the numbers for Miles. And whose turn is it today to meet Hakeem at the train station so nobody fucks with him?"

"It's your turn," says 9-mm.

"Okay. I'll help Ginger and you, Big Wolf, ride with her to the hospital and I'll meet up with you guys later after I meet up with Hakeem at the station."

The 125th Street station is strangely quiet today when I go to meet Hakeem. He'll probably say that he doesn't need the escort any more. And I think these hoods are finally getting the message don't fuck with him. The ghetto is loaded with bastard babies, throwaways, who morph into transformer parasites, cannibals who feed on their own kind. They're troubled by deep insecurities, of course, which they think they're hiding, even from themselves, underneath their gang tattoos and cheap gym muscles. As Hakeem comes out of the train station I'm reminded again why he's a target. He sticks out like a Playboy Bunny in an old folks' home. In his shiny brown shoes, pressed navy blue pants and backpack full of books he is fresh meat. He greets me with a high five and a light kiss on the cheek. Hakeem is the funny man today, laughing and telling jokes.

"Why are you so happy?"

"Guess."

"I don't know, tell me."

"Just take one guess."

"I don't know. What is it?"

"Come on guess and stop being lazy."

"Ahhhh, you're in another production?"

"That's right. I just got a small part in *The Lion King*, the Broadway musical."

I hug Hakeem, overcome with joy. This guy is going to make it to the promised land soon. The ghetto hasn't killed his hopes and dreams. One of the biggest crimes in the hood, I believe, is the murder of kids' dreams. Hakeem is different, he's talented. He has something real to dream about. And his mother is fierce, nurturing his talent, cheering him on. Hakeem and I walk down the street holding hands, lost in good thoughts when a car pulls up.

"Is that your new boyfriend?"

I turn around and it's Pam pulling to the curb.

"Are you going to introduce me to your babyface boyfriend?"

"Go Hakeem, go now and I'll see you later," I tell him. He hesitates, but walks away.

"Now that was not very nice, was it? I like little boys too. Now get your ass in the back of this car before I arrest your ass for being a pedophile!"

I look down the street at Hakeem to make sure he's walking home and wave for him to keep walking when he turns to look back. I get into the car and Pam pulls off bitching.

"Why have you not been answering my calls? Listen. Don't try and flake out on me now because it's not going to work. Be careful or I will have your little boyfriend locked up on Rikers being passed around to a different thug every night."

"He doesn't have anything to do with this."

"You should have thought about that before you had him join a gang. Now he's liable to become state property."

"Just please leave him alone, Pam."

"Or what! What are you going to do? Bitch you are in the back of a police car carrying a gun, money, numbers on you and you know too much, bitch. You lucky I didn't take your little friend for a ride too. You know how many young black boys like him I have put on Rikers Island and they are ruined for life now? Well he's next if you don't show up for this dress rehearsal tonight."

Is Pam playing a part or is she just evil?

"Where are you taking me?"

"Where you want to go?"

"Home."

"Home? Bitch this is not *The Wizard of Oz* and your name is not Dorothy. Look around you. You see a yellow brick road anywhere around here? I feel you, but it's too late for fairy tales. Those days were over for you the moment you started a gang."

Pam heads towards the Bronx. Knowing this crazy bitch this could very well be my last ride. I sneak my phone out, trying to text Hakeem. I want to call Miles but can't at this moment. What the fuck was I thinking fucking with the police in the first place?

"What are you doing? Stop texting now bitch! Put that fucking phone up now!"

"What are you afraid I'm doing Pam, calling the police?"

I put the phone away and look out the window wondering if I will be able to shoot my way out of this. But I think shit like that only happens in movies. She exits in the South Bronx in a warehouse area. As she drives the area becomes darker and more desolate.

"How are you doing back there baby girl? You are not saying much. Are you all right?"

"You're sick bitch, yo."

"But I'm a smart sick bitch who has you locked in the back of my car, taking you to that house on the hill. How do you like it around here? This is where I take my friends when we become enemies. So tell me boo, have you been naughty or nice? Come on, speak up. This is your last chance before we get to that house on the hill."

It's starting to get really dark now and I don't see a soul in sight, only one abandoned warehouse after another. I'm sick to my stomach, as I feel the end is near. Pam pulls over and stops the car. She looks at me in the rear view mirror not saying anything, tying knots in my gut. I want to cry but I can't give this sick bitch the pleasure.

"You can cry you know. No one would know about it but me and you."

"Fuck you."

Pam looks back in her rear view mirror again. Following her eyes I see a black SUV slowly driving towards us. Pam laughs.

"What's going on?"

She doesn't answer. The SUV pulls over and parks directly behind us, but no one gets out of the car.

"What's going on?" Still, she doesn't respond.

I keep looking back at the black SUV trying to keep my composure, but I'm so afraid that my hands and feet are shaking. Finally Pam gets out of the car and opens the door of the building behind us. Trouble and Cognac emerge from the SUV with chainsaws. Pam walks back to my window and opens it slightly as Trouble walks up to the window and throws some kind of smoke bomb inside, immediately causing me to choke and tear up. As I go to grab my gun the door opens and I'm pulled out of the car. As they drag me inside the warehouse I see Pam cutting on the chainsaw. They drag me to the back of the warehouse and hold me down.

"Who have you been talking to bitch?" Pam yells at me holding the up chainsaw.

"Now I'm going to ask you again and don't lie to me. Who did you tell about the restaurant?"

"No one. I swear to God!"

"Enough lies bitch, it's over."

Pam slowly raises the chainsaw to my face. I can smell the gasoline as the sawblade comes close to my face. I try to break away but can't. Pam holds the spinning blade up to my face, I pray that I pass out so I won't feel a thing. Suddenly Pam cuts off the chainsaw and backs away. Trouble and Cognac let me go and step away.

"Like I said. I could have put Hakeem in the back of the car with you and both of your heads could be laying on the floor right now. Show up on at the salon for the robbery on Saturday or I guarantee that you and Hakeem are going to get a free ride to that house on the hill."

I don't know how I found a gypsy cab, but when it pulls up to my building I think this fucking building is looking sweeter and sweeter every day. Happiness can be found in the simplest things in life. Happiness could be found in just being alive. I enter the funky elevator that is always running on time, not quite, but you know what I mean. I walk inside and see Pinch is not so damn ugly after all. Pinch is okay. She's alright. I don't think she has a bad bone in her body. She always gives out Miles' liquor for free and is always trying to help these drunk mothafuckas get home safe, except when she can't because she's high herself. But that doesn't happen too often. Pinch looks at me and smiles.

"What's going on baby girl? How was your day?"

She walks over and gives me a hug, which is all I need. Miles walks in from the kitchen smelling like fried catfish. He puts on some Gospel music that I never heard sound so good. Miles walks over to us singing and grabs me and Pinch. He starts to clap his hands and says, "Come on ladies let's go to church up in here."

Miles starts dancing around clapping and singing, me and Pinch follow his lead and start clapping our hands and dancing around. Miles turns up the volume of the music. He comes back to us and begins to preach as me and Pinch sing and march around in a circle. Joy comes back into my heart as we sing our Harlem blues away.

Dear God, I think that Miles saved me the other night. If I'm still alive by the end of this day I will have to change my life or at best I will end up like my mother in some upstate prison. Hakeem is waiting for me downstairs. I told him that I had to speak with him.

"I don't like that cop. She seemed a little weird to me, that way she was staring, she gave me the creeps," he says.

"Like I told you if she ever comes around, run, stay away from her… you got it?"

He shakes his head okay.

"Listen, I have to go now, but promise me you are going to focus on your acting no matter what."

"Yeah of course I already told you that, no worries."

"I mean it. No matter what."

"What's wrong? Why are you acting so morbid?"

"It's nothing." I hug him and walk away. In the cab I review Pam's plans and the blue print sketch of the salon in my head. I think I have everything, Jericho, the bag and the plastic cuffs. I've been going over this shit so many times now with those mothafuckas that my brain is numb. As I get to the location, I see Trouble and Cognac waiting on the corner smoking cigarettes. Trouble is already on the very edge.

"Bitch you are ten minutes late."

I don't bother to answer him as we walk to Nicky's place. When get there a big guy in a suit is walking in. We put on our ski masks, draw our guns and follow him in. When they interview the victims some of them will say he was part of the gang. Cognac yells.

"Nobody moves, nobody gets shot."

A woman next to me screams, so I smack her. Trouble locks the door and closes the blinds. I run to the back of the salon and check the men's bathroom, all clear. I go into the women's bathroom and this big, fat, black, smelly bitch with curls in her hair is taking a shit on the toilet. It smells like something crawled inside her and died. I yell, "Get yo funky ass up."

I run over and pull this stinky bitch off the toilet. The smell almost knocks me out. She pulls her panties up and I push her out of the bathroom. I see Pam with her hands up and her hair half done coming to the back with about twelve other women laced in expensive jewelry. Trouble is also pushing two big black guys in suits with their hands cuffed behind their backs, into the back room. In the back of the salon we tell everyone to lie down on their stomachs. One guy is taking too long, so Trouble pushes him down. I see Cognac taking Pam into the office. I grab the closest female to me, turn her over and raise my gun butt to knock her teeth out like Pam said, but she looks like one of those NBA wives and too pretty to hit. So I grab the fat bitch from the bathroom and smack her in the mouth with the gun knocking out some teeth.

She hollers, "Don't kill me please, don't kill me!"

"Shut the fuck up!"

Trouble tells me to hurry and take all the jewelry off the bitches.

"Yeah bitches you heard the man, take your shit off."

I go to one bitch after the other taking their shit. I go to Pam to take her shit and she pushes my hands away, so I go to the next rich bitch. Trouble puts blindfolds on the big guys on the floor, when two male hair stylists open the back door, walk inside exhaling cigarette smoke. They see people on the floor and scream. I look over to them waving my gun.

"Get your asses on the floor."

I lean down and cuff their hands behind their backs. I open the big metal back door and there are two more hairdressers smoking, unaware of the robbery going on inside. When I throw the two women back inside, I see Pam standing up and rushing to the front. As Cognac opens the front door with the bag of money in his hands, Pam pulls out her gun and shoots him. Trouble turns and returns fire. I'm totally confused, wondering what the hell is going on. The bitches on the floor panic, screaming at the top of their lungs. The fat bitch jumps up and runs into the bathroom. Pam and Trouble are shooting at each other. I'm fucking stunned. I hear Jericho screaming! "Shoot that bitch in the back and run!" Pam shoots Trouble in the face then turns and shoots at me. I freak out and drop Jericho on the floor, idiot! I reach for my snub 32 and realize I left it at the house. I grab one of those NBA bitches and hide behind her as a shield. Pam runs toward us pointing her gun, I'm dead, I know it, this bitch set us all up. I should have left town, but it's too late now. I'll be leaving the hood alright but not the way I had planned. Pam is only a few feet away and I'm a few feet away from death when I see 9-mm walk through the door blasting. I was wondering what was taking him so long. I had told my crew to come in as soon as they heard gunfire. Pam looks back and jumps over a counter. I grab the bag and Jericho from the floor and run towards the front door. As I run past the counter, Pam fires at me. I return fire as she ducks down behind the counter. I run over Trouble's body then Cognac's, as Big Wolf grabs the money bag from Cognac's hands. Outside I see Switchblade driving slowly past. We hit the back of the van running. Big Wolf closes the door as Pam continues firing from the middle of the street. Switchblade turns the corner and we head down to Spanish Harlem to 9-mm uncle's garage on 104th and 5th Ave. I ask if everyone is okay and where is Missy Capone. Wolf says she's lying in the cut watching the hair salon.

"You guys timed that shit perfectly. I knew that bitch was setting us up."

"But why all this drama?" Big Wolf says. "Why not kill your ass in the Bronx when she had a chance, cause that shit back there was crazy and a mess. TKO, we have to get you out of town, Pam is coming for you. She has to try and kill you for sure." Wolf opens the bag filled with cash.

"Yeah baby, we got this."

We drive up to the garage on 104th Street. 9-mm jumps out to open the garage door. Foxy Red is inside the garage, waiting for us, talking on her cell phone. We all jump out of the van, 9-mm and Wolf take out razors, immediately cutting off the blue plastic skin that is covering the brown van. Foxy Red hands me a plane ticket to Houston, Texas. "You okay?" she asks. "Your flight leaves tomorrow at 7:30 in the evening. You can tell your Uncle Leroy that he can pick you up at the airport at 12:30 just after midnight."

How does she know about my Uncle Leroy? She hands me five debit cards.

"Here are debit cards for different accounts I've set up for you. Including the money from the robbery, you should have enough cash to live on for at least a year. I have a place for us to stay on East 82nd Street until you are ready to leave tomorrow. I have your packed suitcase there as well." My cell phone rings and it's Missy Capone saying there's a squadron of cops at the hair salon and that the TV is showing people getting oxygen.

Wolf and 9-mm put the blue plastic skin in black garbage bags, then put the original plates back on the van and take off the bulletproof glass taped to the van's back windows. We empty the contents of both bags onto a clear plastic sheet and see what we have in cash and jewelry. I get another call, saying Pam is outside getting oxygen. I think to myself that bitch don't need any oxygen, she needs some oxazolidinone that bitch. And they need to inject that shit directly into her brains, that's the only way it will work. We count the money and put the jewelry in a box to hide in it in the abandoned building for the time being. Missy Capone texts to say she's on her way. She's so excited when she walks through the door she's almost dancing.

"There are cops all over the place, helicopters flying all low over the projects looking for mothafuckas."

"Why is it when shit like this happens, they go straight to the projects?" 9-mm complains. "Like everyone in the projects is involved in crime."

"Well I'm from the projects and I'm involved in a whole lot of mothafuckin crime," I say and everyone laughs.

"Let's wrap this up and go our separate ways. We'll meet later at the basement."

Switchblade is watching NY1 on her iPhone.

"Damn that shit is crazy uptown, cops and shit everywhere! There are so many people standing across the street from the salon you would think they were having a concert out there. I tell you they are looking all over the place for you out there. You are going to have to hide among the graves or something, that's the only place where they won't be looking for you."

It's time for me to change clothes. I get into costume, a tight dress, high heels, a long wig, red lipstick and a purse. Foxy Red and I put on big sunglasses and leave. We walk to the corner and hail a cab. A gypsy African cab driver pulls over and we tell him to go to 96th Street. We walk south a block and this time hail a yellow cab. We direct the driver to East 84th Street and Park Avenue. The driver starts to talk to us immediately.

"I just came from Harlem. There are police everywhere, all over West Harlem. There was a robbery at a fancy beauty salon. They say three robbers came in with guns blazing and robbed and killed people, but there was an off duty cop there who started shooting back and killed two of the suspects. The third suspect got away in a blue van with fifteen thousand in cash and over two hundred thousand dollars' worth of jewelry. The radio said there were wives of NBA players there who were pistol whipped before they were robbed. You know that must be a terrible scene. Dead bodies, blood and shit all over the place. My God man! What has America come to? When I came here from Senegal , I thought this was the place of milk and honey, not smoking guns, body bags and blood."

"I hear you," I say looking out the window and behind me.

"You can drop us off on the near corner of 84th and Park."

Our destination is really East 84th Street and East End Avenue. As we walk I get a text. "You are a dead bitch! You won't live to see another day." Moments later I get another threatening text. What happened to this wicked witch to make her so depraved? She suffers from moral rot festering the deepest corners of her mind. I'm aware that I'm the last person who can get caught up in morality and shit but damn, that bitch is the female Satan. Or maybe she is Satan, in disguise. The Devil can turn himself into anything. As we enter the large elegant apartment Foxy Red brings me back to reality.

"There are cold cuts in the refrigerator. I'll make us some sandwiches. Are you hungry?"

"Hell yeah, I forgot to eat this morning, that's how freaked out I was when I woke up. I didn't know if I would be dead or alive by this time. But y'all did a great job executing that game plan. You should have seen that bitch's face when 9-mm came through that door with guns on fire. That's right bitch! Now my soldiers are setting some asses on fire."

Foxy looks me up and down.

"You look totally different wearing a dress, makeup, lipstick and long hair. I would not have recognized you like that if I had passed you on the street."

"Good I'm glad you said that, because it means that I have a better chance of leaving this town alive."

Later in the evening Foxy Red and I head to the basement for a last meeting of the gang before I leave for Texas. We don't take any chances and walk down a back alley behind the apartment. The first thing we hear is the rats running, scratching, chattering. As quickly as we can we get to Big Wolf's apartment and bang on the door, Missy Capone opens it.

"Let go yo." She locks the door behind us.

"Is everyone here?" I ask, feeling a little nervous.

"Yeah, just about."

We walk into the living room and my crew is watching the news on their cell phones. I pace. Switchblade tells me what they're saying.

"They are looking for a very young black male suspect, or possibly a young, black female, fifteen to eighteen years old. And another black male between the ages of eighteen to twenty two, wearing a black jacket with a hoodie and brown boots, who got away in a blue van. They're asking anyone with any information to call crime stoppers immediately."

"I've stashed everything in the hiding place a few buildings down," Switchblade says. "Fucking cops everywhere. TKO it's time for you to disappear. Me and the whole crew except Red and Hakeem are going upstate to my grandmother's house for a few days to lay low. She has been trying to get me to paint her house for the past year so me and the crew are going to do that now."

"I told you to take Hakeem with you."

"He said his mother doesn't want to leave, but said he talked her into going to his aunt's house in Jersey for a few days and they are leaving sometime tonight."

"Make sure they get to Jersey tonight and don't tell him anything about what happened, I will call him when I get to Texas."

"We'll make sure he gets to and from school safely every day," says Missy.

"You all know what to do while I'm gone. Just stick to the game plan and everything is going to be fine. I should be back within the next six months or so. I want everybody to stay out of trouble until I get back. We will be talking on the phone every day. It's time for everyone to man and woman up now. That's how you can handle it."

Switchblade grabs me with tears in her eyes. She hugs me and says, "You look beautiful with that dress on. I'm going to miss you. Stay away from trouble in Texas. Email us your new phone number as soon as you get there."

"No problem, of course. I'll text you as soon as I get there.

I hug her again.

"Missy Capone. Do the right thing now. It's up to you to lead the gang and to make the right decisions. And remember, don't touch the jewelry and try and sell it. That shit will only bring heat and lots of trouble, prison trouble. You don't have to go to prison to get some kind of street cred, don't let some of these rappers educate you into thinking you have to be as dumb as they are in order to survive. You have these foreigners coming to America every day who grow up drinking muddy water and whose children had to walk miles to school with no shoes, but yet when they come here they send their kids to college. We are growing up with shoes on, blocks from City College and Columbia University, but we travel miles away and go to college on Rikers Island. I'm not going to be around to talk y'all out of doing something stupid! Think bitches think! Slow your roll. Go to Barnes and Noble. Sit your asses down and read some books. That's all I have to say to you before I leave, now the shit is on you."

If only I had taken my own advice! I look at my crew one last time wondering what will become of them when I'm gone. Scarface Pretty, who is always quick as a mouse, looks a little shocked right now that I'm leaving. But there is nothing I can do. I hug the whole crew, say goodbye to yesterday where all of my troubles were always up in my face. I turn and Foxy Red and I walk out the door.

ELEVEN

Dear God,

I have a confession. I DON'T WANT TO DIE! I will do anything
to live. That's what I know. Life, even my life is precious. As long
as I breathe I can change. Maybe when I leave this city I'll be able
to really come to the light. I want to live, Dear God and if that
means I want to be redeemed, praise your name!

I've been talking to Miles on the phone and he keeps saying
that he has a funny feeling that I had something to do with
the robbery at the salon and that's why I have to leave the city
all of a sudden. And of course I deny everything. The only
people who know my sins and secrets are my crew, Pam and
the two dead men. Foxy Red is trying to get my attention. She
wants to order some food and she's waving a stack of menus
in front of my face. I don't want her to hear me talking to
Miles.

"Gotta go, Uncle Miles. You'll be hearing from me. I'll be
back to collect for you."

The food arrives and we eat in front of the TV in the den.
We turn to New York 1 to get an update from crime scene. A
female reporter is at the salon talking about the robbery and
calling Pam a hero for killing two of the suspects and saving

customers inside Nicky's. The reporter says the police believe the suspects were also involved in the robbery and murders of the family at Giorgio's, because they found the murder weapon on one of the suspects. They believe that the suspect found out about the restaurant that Pam worked security for through his girlfriend, who worked at the salon. The girlfriend is being held by the police for questioning. The reporter also says also says that Pam will no doubt be promoted to the rank of Detective for her heroics, stopping the robbery as she was getting her hair done. She also said that the police are looking for a third suspect who got away with money and thousands of dollars worth of jewelry. They believe the suspect was also involved in the robbery and murder at Giorgio's. The suspect is described as a baby faced killer, a young black male or female about five feet four, a hundred and ten pounds, between the ages of sixteen and twenty years old.

Wow. Foxy Red and I look at each other in disbelief.

She says, "All that was to set you guys up to take the hit for the murders downtown. That's why she tried to kill you too. That way she gets away with the murder and walks away a hero with a promotion. That's a crazy calculating bitch! She would be brilliant in politics. If she gets away with this, she is going places in life. She is not going to leave any stones unturned looking for you. I'm afraid Missy Capone is right. The only place you will be able to hide is among the graves."

I think to myself that's not good when you have to hide out among deep people. That's not the kind of company I like to keep. Lord, I always knew I was going to die young, but not like this, on the run from a crazy police bitch who was turning me out on a regular basis, having me give her head as she held a gun to my face. Shit like this is only supposed to happen in the movies. But then again my life is a movie, I'm like Billy the Kid, an outlaw on the run packing two six guns. My wanted poster is on television around the world. "Wanted with two bullets between the eyes."

I still find it hard to believe what Pam tried to do to me. I trusted her at first because I thought she was going to help me rehabilitate myself. And then I thought she really liked me. Loved me. That's how needy I am. I played a role in the drama that she writes about her life. She cast me as the goat. But I'm bowing out of the show. This series is cancelled. My next role will be in a fairy tale where dreams come true, in a place where I don't have to worry about getting my head blown off. I guess I'm going to Disneyland y'all.

As my phone rings I know it's Hakeem. He's been trying me all day.

"Are you really leaving New York?"

"Yes. But it's best for you not to know where I'm going baby and no worries. The gang will be around to protect you."

"I want to protect you now Jean."

"I'll see you baby. Take care."

Foxy Red doesn't give me any time to be sentimental. She's all business.

"We need to figure out in more detail the direction of the gang and the expansion of drug business TKO. I know you love you some Hakeem, but we need to keep our cash coming."

She's talking like a real gang banger now, but I don't comment about that.

"Love Hakeem? Bitch are you out of your mind? Bitch I'm gay!"

"You are only sixteen. You don't know what you are and don't tell me you and Hakeem never had sex."

"Of course not, we never had sex! And why are you worried about my sex life for anyway?"

"Why are you getting so defensive? This is not a personal attack on you, I was only making an observation. I was thinking you were gay because that's the trendy thing to do now."

"Listen I'm not following any trend and I don't give a damn about no male niggas in America, especially Hakeem okay! So can we discuss some real business and not this bullshit you're talking about!"

"Not a problem… so how should we handle things while you're in Texas?"

"Wait about six months to sell the jewelry when the shit has died down and nobody is looking for it to show up anyplace. I know a jeweler down on West 47th Street we can sell it to. The cash from the robbery, I want you to keep most of it to expand the business. It's time for us to get out of this nickel and dime petty drug dealing shit. We need to invest that money and go into the wholesale drug game. Wholesale is where the real money's at. We gonna wholesale powdered crack cocaine, heroin, marijuana, oxycodone, ecstasy and BZP. You'll also need to recruit more loyal mercenaries. If we're going to go big we need a lot more foot soldiers in the field. We need bodies to sling that amount of weight. If these mothafuckas are going to church on Sundays, they need to be smoking our crack and sniffing our coke on Mondays. If niggas gonna praise God during the day, we need to have them worshipping the devil at night."

Foxy looks at me. "Do you want some more food?"

"Yeah I'll take some more food." I look at this half Jewish red bitch and see a true gangsta bitch. I don't see no player hating or jealousy, only loyalty and respect. The biggest disease the hood needs a cure for is not high blood pressure or diabetes, but hater-aids and insecurities. Foxy Red looks at me with tenderly and drops her bomb.

"I think we should get rid of Pam without all the fireworks. We should take her out like we did Snake, but without the blood and guts."

"What do you suggest?"

"You said Pam loves young girls and getting head right?"

"Yeah she does."

Foxy looks around thinking.

"On second thought, fuck that complicated bullshit! We need to take a lesson from what happened with Snake. We should just blow her head off and call it a night! Because I think she is coming after all of us. We know too much and that's way too many loose ends for her."

"When and where do you think we should do it? Because I'm already gone."

"That's going to be easy. We'll be in the crowd at her promotion ceremony with the Mayor and Commissioner. And when she gets into her car to leave, we do a drive by with silencers on the gun, professional style."

I look at Red and laugh. Is this what she learns at Stuyvesant High School? This red bitch can't be serious. She looks at me and doesn't flinch.

"I'm serious. That's the last place she would expect us to be. We need to take her out in her own back yard! What do we have to lose? She is out there now looking for us. Fuck it! The day she is promoted to Detective is the day she dies!"

I think when I come back to New York in a year or so I won't have to fight Missy Capone or Scarface to get back control of the gang again. I see now, it's gonna be this red bitch, who is not from some hood and who didn't grow up in a bad environment, whose momma is a conservative Jewish bitch and whose father is a Clarence Thomas. I see now this bitch is going to be a formidable adversary. She's going into the lion's den to take out Pam and she is super smart. She will be running circles around Switchblade, Missy Capone and Scarface Pretty in no time. And I see how Big Wolf and 9-mm Rottweiler tongues are wiggling out of their mouths whenever this fine pretty red bitch is around. So they have already been compromised and co-opted. And just minutes ago I thought her concern for me was based on loyalty and respect. She's just trying to find out how stupid I am. She looks at me.

"You look so very attractive like that. Why do girls like you go around dressed like guys? You don't like guys, and yet you dress like one. To me love and hate can't coexist in the same space, there's an internal conflict there. Do you ever feel conflicted?"

"Bitch! What is your problem! Are you applying for the job to be my psychologist or something? Maybe you haven't heard, but I've been having a very bad day and you are sitting over there trying to psychoanalyze me."

I stand up, march to the bathroom pissed off. I lock the bathroom door behind me and stare in the mirror trying to compose myself.

I wake up on East 82nd Street, so I'm still alive, but I can't wait until tonight when I'm on that plane heading to Texas. It's too much drama in the city for me now. I'm wanted with a bullet in my head and toe tags on both feet. In the bathroom, I brush my teeth, shower and do my hair and makeup in the mirror. I put on my dress and boots and sunglasses and look at my reflection. I look like a glamorous Hollywood movie star. "I'm ready for my close up now Mr. Spielberg." I put on more red lipstick, walk out the door, check my bags and I'm ready to go. I still can't believe I'm leaving and that I made it this far. By the grace of God and great grandmama watching over me I'm still here. In a few hours, I'll be on the plane on my way to a new land, to a new day dawning and the promise of a better tomorrow. All that bullshit which now sounds pretty good to me. I know I'm one of the lucky ones, because most of the Indians never get a chance to leave the reservation.

Foxy Red walks into the room wearing a beautiful flowered dress that reminds me of the dresses I used to wear as a child.

"It's time to go now. The car is downstairs waiting to take us to the airport."

I grab my suitcase and look at myself one more time in the mirror. I notice how my breasts stick out now. Before I always wore a type of girdle to suppress my breasts and butt. Now it's all hanging out and the ass is looking rounder and sticking out more than J-Lo's. But we black women always have been known for our fabulous big round asses, from the very moment we stepped off the slave ships. So how in the hell did we let J-Lo and Kim Kardashian not only get credit, but make millions of dollars on our shit? I remember seeing old photographs of black women with glasses of water resting on their asses to showcase their freakish size. Now big money is involved showcasing fat asses, and we are nowhere to be seen. What kind of shit is that? We are not even runners up in the big ass contest. Hello somebody... What is wrong with this picture? I'm not talking about no damn strippers in some fucking club. I'm talking about the commercialization of ass and how we are nowhere in that picture. Say it loud ladies, "I got ass and I'm proud." Now shake that ass and snap your fingers and say it loud, "I got ass and I'm proud!" I'm riffing again. I'm anxious.

In the lobby the doorman grabs my suitcase, but I keep my handbag with my guns in it. I'm not giving up my guns until we get to the airport and I'm ready to walk through the detector. I'm not out of New York or harm's way yet, so I put my hand inside my bag and hold Jericho. My snub nose 32 is resting on its side next to Jericho. As we walk to the car I notice a black car that was parked down the street suddenly pull off, heading in our direction. Oh shit! I hear Jericho starting to kick and scream. A flock of pigeons on the sidewalk takes flight at the same moment and I jump. As our driver grabs my luggage and opens the trunk, the car is almost on us and I can see a young black female behind the wheel who looks like Pam. My God, she's reaching for a gun. I push Foxy Red back and I drop my bag, holding both guns as the car approaches. I raise my guns getting ready to start blasting. The bitch in the car shrieks. It's not Pam. I quickly turn putting my guns down and back into the bag on the ground. Our driver takes his head out of the trunk.

"What happened? Who's screaming?" Foxy and I jump into the back of the car. Finally the driver closes the trunk, gets into the front seat and drives away. Foxy and I laugh and every time we stop laughing we start again. Nervous laughter. Crazy laughter. Why ARE these two crazy bitches laughing? Why? Because we are going to make it out of the city and I'm still alive. I will miss New York, Miles, Pinch and my whole crew. I just wonder how I'm going to go from selling drugs and running numbers to living with my Uncle and his Christian family in Texas. I know I'll get my GED and I guess I'll read a lot of books to pass the time. It's better to be bored and alive in Texas than dead somewhere in New York.

We are on the road and it doesn't look like I will be going to the morgue today. Foxy Red and I look at each other and laugh again. She gives me a high five and despite my doubts about her I hug her tight. We hold each other in the back of the car. I'm happy and I'm sad. This is the end of my New York life for now. As we approach the highway I look back at the city one last time. It's possible that I might not see her ever again. It's possible, but not likely.

TO BE CONTINUED